D0951935

Match Wits with Super Sleuth Nancy Drew!

Collect the Original
Nancy Drew Mystery Stories®
by Carolyn Keene

Available in Hardcover!

The Secret of the Old Clock
The Hidden Staircase
The Bungalow Mystery
The Mystery at Lilac Inn
The Secret of Shadow Ranch
The Secret of Red Gate Farm
The Clue in the Diary
Nancy's Mysterious Letter
The Sign of the Twisted Candles
Password to Larkspur Lane
The Clue of the Broken Locket
The Message in the Hollow Oak
The Mystery of the Ivory Charm
The Whispering Statue
The Haunted Bridge
The Clue of the Tapping Heels
The Mystery of the Brass-Bound
  Trunk
The Mystery of the Moss-Covered
  Mansion
The Quest of the Missing Map
The Clue in the Jewel Box
The Secret in the Old Attic
The Clue in the Crumbling Wall
The Mystery of the Tolling Bell
The Clue in the Old Album
The Ghost of Blackwood Hall
The Clue of the Leaning Chimney
The Secret of the Wooden Lady

The Clue of the Black Keys
Mystery at the Ski Jump
The Clue of the Velvet Mask
The Ringmaster's Secret
The Scarlet Slipper Mystery
The Witch Tree Symbol
The Hidden Window Mystery
The Haunted Showboat
The Secret of the Golden Pavilion
The Clue in the Old Stagecoach
The Mystery of the Fire Dragon
The Clue of the Dancing Puppet
The Moonstone Castle Mystery
The Clue of the Whistling Bagpipes
The Phantom of Pine Hill
The Mystery of the 99 Steps
The Clue in the Crossword Cipher
The Spider Sapphire Mystery
The Invisible Intruder
The Mysterious Mannequin
The Crooked Banister
The Secret of Mirror Bay
The Double Jinx Mystery
Mystery of the Glowing Eye
The Secret of the Forgotten City
The Sky Phantom
Strange Message in the Parchment
Mystery of Crocodile Island
The Thirteenth Pearl

Nancy Drew Back-to-Back
The Secret of the Old Clock/ The Hidden Staircase

Celebrate 60 Years with the World's Best Detective!

THE CLUE IN THE OLD ALBUM

Nancy Drew witnesses a purse snatching and runs after the thief. She rescues the purse, but not its contents, then is asked by the owner, a doll collector, to do some detective work.

"The source of light will heal all ills, but a curse will follow him who takes it from the gypsies."

This is one of the clues Nancy is given to find an old album, a lost doll, and a missing gypsy violinist. The young sleuth never gives up her search, though she is poisoned by a French-swordsman doll, run off the road in her car by an enemy, and sent many warnings to give up the case.

Fans will enjoy Nancy's clever ways of finding all she seeks, and bringing happiness to a misunderstood child and her lonely grandmother.

"Nancy has been poisoned!" the doctor announced.

NANCY DREW MYSTERY STORIES®

The Clue in the Old Album

BY CAROLYN KEENE

GROSSET & DUNLAP
Publishers • New York
A member of The Putnam & Grosset Group

PRINTED ON RECYCLED PAPER

Acknowledgement is made to Mildred Wirt Benson, who under the pen name
Carolyn Keene, wrote the original NANCY DREW books

Contents

CHAPTER		PAGE
I	A STOLEN PURSE	1
II	THE DOLL COLLECTOR	10
III	NANCY'S ASSIGNMENT	18
IV	THE CHILD BRIDE	29
V	FOILED	39
VI	UPSETTING NEWS	49
VII	A HELPFUL GIFT	61
VIII	THE FORTUNETELLER'S TRICK	70
IX	A STRANGE DISMISSAL	78
X	COMPLICATIONS	87
XI	A WARNING	95
XII	AN INTERRUPTED PROGRAM	108
XIII	A STRANGE PRESENT	115
XIV	THE MANNEQUIN'S HINT	125
XV	A DETECTIVE FAILS	132
XVI	THE TELEVISION CLUE	140
XVII	DOUBLE DISAPPEARANCE	146
XVIII	AN UNEXPECTED REUNION	157
XIX	THE SOURCE-OF-LIGHT DOLL	165
XX	TWO VICTORIES	174

The Clue in the Old Album

CHAPTER I

A Stolen Purse

THUNDEROUS applause echoed through the
crowded concert hall of the River Heights Art
Museum.

"Oh, Dad, isn't the violinist marvelous?" Nancy
Drew whispered to her father. "The gypsy music
he just played—"

A hush came over the audience as Alfred Blackwell tucked his violin under his chin. When he
began the melody, Nancy was startled by a stifled
sob from a white-haired woman who sat across the
aisle. She was listening with rapt attention and
tears rolled down her cheeks.

Nancy also saw something else. A dark-haired
man on the aisle seat next to the woman reached
for a jeweled purse that lay unguarded in her lap.
Slyly he dropped it into his pocket, got up, and
started quickly for the lobby.

"Dad, that man's a thief!" Nancy whispered. "I'm going after him!"

Before Mr. Drew could recover from his surprise, Nancy had scrambled past him and hurried up the aisle after the thief. He pushed past an usher and fled into the lobby. Nancy reached it a moment later, but the thief was out of sight.

Doorways opened into corridors in three directions and led to various exhibition rooms. Nancy chose the nearest one. The only person in sight was a watchman.

"Did a man in evening clothes come this way just now?" she asked.

"No one's been through here in the past twenty minutes, miss."

"He stole a jeweled purse! Please help me catch him!"

"You bet I will!"

The guard hurried into the second corridor and Nancy took the third. As she rounded a turn, she saw the thief far ahead. He had stopped to examine the purse.

"Drop that!" Nancy cried out, running toward him.

The man pulled out the contents, flung the bag away, and darted through a door opening into an alley. Nancy snatched up the purse, then resumed the chase. The alley was dark and she could not see the man. Disappointed, but aware that it was hopeless to pursue him, she turned back.

"Drop that purse!" Nancy cried out.

From the museum lobby came the sound of voices. Among a group of people Nancy saw the guard. Behind him were her father and the elderly lady whose bag she had retrieved.

When the woman saw the purse in Nancy's hand, she exclaimed, "Oh, I'm so thankful you recovered my bag. The contents are precious to me."

"I'm sorry the thief escaped," Nancy said. "And I'm afraid he took whatever was inside the purse."

She handed it over. Nervously the woman opened the bag. It was indeed empty!

"Oh, my money is gone! And a letter and a photograph that mean a great deal to me!" she cried.

"I'll call the police," the guard offered.

"No!" the woman insisted. "Thank you, but I do not want any publicity."

Mr. Drew said the authorities should be notified. "No thief should be allowed to go free."

"Very well," the woman agreed reluctantly. "I suppose the report must be made in my name. I am Mrs. John Struthers of Kenwood Drive."

Mr. Drew asked if she could identify the purse snatcher.

"I scarcely noticed him," she confessed.

Nancy spoke up. "He was about thirty years old with a mottled complexion and piercing black eyes. He walked with a slight stoop and wore evening clothes that were too large for him."

"You're observant, miss," the guard said. "Come to think of it, I know a fellow who looks like that. Let me see—it must have been when I was custodian at the bank. Yes, that's it."

"He worked there?" Nancy asked, amazed.

"No. He used to come in to see one of the tellers. They got mixed up in some crooked scheme. The teller was fired. I don't know what happened to his buddy, but I heard he was a professional pickpocket."

"How long ago was that?" Mr. Drew asked the custodian.

"Six months or more. Excuse me. I'll phone the police."

Mrs. Struthers had regained her poise but a faraway look had come into her eyes. "If it hadn't been for that gypsy music—" She broke off as if she regretted having revealed something.

The woman turned to Nancy and added, "I am very remiss. I haven't thanked you for all your trouble, and I really am most appreciative. May I know your name?"

"Nancy Drew," the strawberry blond, blue-eyed girl replied. "And this is my father," she added, introducing tall, handsome Carson Drew.

Mrs. Struthers smiled and said, "I see now why it was you, Nancy, who spotted the thief. You are often written up in the papers for your cleverness in tracking down unscrupulous people."

Nancy laughed, brushing aside the compliment.

She asked if the Drews could be of any further help to Mrs. Struthers.

"I believe not, thank you," the woman replied. "I must find my granddaughter, Rose, who came with me. We were invited to Madame Mazorka's reception for Mr. Blackwell. But I hadn't planned to go on account of Rose."

"You really shouldn't miss it," Nancy said. She felt that the social affair might take the woman's mind off her loss. "Perhaps—"

The young detective's remark was cut short by a strikingly pretty girl of about twelve years of age, who unexpectedly pirouetted among them. Coal-black wavy hair fell to her shoulders and dark eyes sparkled brightly, though they looked as if they were capable of blazing with temper.

Mrs. Struthers said to the Drews, "I should like you to meet my granddaughter Rose."

"Hi," Rose said as she finished her dance with a pert curtsy. "Wasn't the recital super?"

"It certainly was, Rose," Nancy remarked. "I'm thrilled that we're going to Madame Mazorka's to meet Mr. Blackwell."

"We've been invited, too, so we can all go together!" Rose suggested.

"Please, dear," Mrs. Struthers remonstrated. "Perhaps the Drews have other plans. We can take a cab."

"We'd be delighted to have you ride with us," Mr. Drew said. "I'll get the car."

Without waiting for the others, Rose went along with him and hopped into the front seat. While she chatted gaily with Mr. Drew, Mrs. Struthers sat in the back with Nancy and confided to the girl that she would like her assistance in solving a mystery.

"Would it be possible, my dear, for you to come to tea at my home tomorrow afternoon?" Mrs. Struthers asked eagerly. "I'd like to talk to you privately."

"I'd love to. May I bring a dear friend along? She often helps me on cases."

The woman agreed and suggested that they meet at four o'clock. There was no chance for further conversation as Mr. Drew pulled up in front of Madame Mazorka's home.

The charming hostess received her guests graciously. She introduced them to the violinist. As he shook hands with Nancy, Alfred Blackwell's eyes twinkled. "Are you not the young lady who was carried away by my encore?" he teased.

"That's a very kind way of looking at my interruption," she replied, laughing. "I wish I'd been as skillful in my performance as you were in yours."

As Nancy told the artist she hoped to have the pleasure of hearing him play again soon, Rose suddenly rushed forward. "How about my meeting Mr. Blackwell?"

She shook hands with the musician, then spun

away, twirling dangerously close to a portly gentleman who was trying to carry a plate of sandwiches and a glass of punch in one hand. To the strains of a three-piece orchestra Rose began to dance in the middle of the floor.

Many of the guests were staring coolly at her exhibition. Nancy realized that the best way out of the awkward situation would be for the girl to depart. She turned to the distressed grandmother.

"I believe my father is ready to leave now, Mrs. Struthers," she said. "We'll be glad to take you home."

The woman, greatly relieved to escape, retrieved Rose. After the Drews had left them at their home, Nancy told her father of Mrs. Struthers' invitation to talk over a mystery.

"Have you any idea what it might be?" she asked.

"I've heard very little about Mrs. Struthers," the lawyer said. "I understand she and her granddaughter have lived in River Heights two years. Mrs. Struthers is reputed to be wealthy and has traveled a lot. But it's said she now stays at home all the time. She's sad and very secretive about her affairs."

"It should be an interesting case," Nancy speculated. "I wonder if it could have anything to do with Rose."

"That child should be taught to behave better," Carson Drew declared, frowning.

"Maybe her actions are the result of pent-up energy," Nancy ventured. "Who knows, she may have some hidden talent!"

"Perhaps you're right," Mr. Drew said.

The following day Nancy drove to the Struthers' home, accompanied by slender, attractive George Fayne. She was as excited as Nancy over the prospect of a new mystery.

Nancy parked the car in front of a large brick house, which stood some distance from others in the neighborhood. It was surrounded by lawns and a high iron fence.

The two friends started up the long walk to the front door. Suddenly a shout behind them made Nancy and George turn.

Too late! Before they could tell who or what was coming, the girls were knocked to the ground.

CHAPTER II

The Doll Collector

"HYPERS!" George exclaimed, as she scrambled to her feet and rubbed her knee. "Where'd the cyclone come from?"

Nancy brushed the dirt from her clothes and pointed down the path. Rose was precariously jerking to a halt on a bright-red motorbike. "There's our culprit!"

The young girl hopped off the vehicle and skipped toward them. "Jiminy crickets! When you get up speed on that thing, it's hard to stop," she explained, then added, "I'm sorry if I hurt you."

Nancy assured Rose that fortunately both she and her friend were all right, and introduced Rose to George.

"Aren't you a little young to be riding around on a motorbike?" George asked.

"Regular bikes are too slow," Rose declared.

"I traded mine for this one, but it doesn't work right."

"Does your grandmother approve of your having it?" Nancy asked.

"Granny doesn't approve of anything I do." Rose pouted, then laughed. "She couldn't interfere in this deal. I traded my two-wheeler for this secondhand motorbike before she could say no."

"Your name ought to be Wild Rose," said George, disgusted.

Rose frowned. "You're a meanie. You're a girl and they call you George!"

"Have you a license for the motorbike?" George asked her.

Rose's face grew red. "No."

"Then it's against the law to ride it."

"I'll watch out for the police." Rose giggled. "Say, did you come to see Granny?"

"Yes, she invited us to tea," Nancy replied.

"Well, don't let her get you into her clutches—not with all those funny dolls of hers!" Rose warned.

Before the girls could ask what she meant, Rose ran off to retrieve her motorbike.

"You heard what she said?" George asked in a hushed voice. "Maybe we're heading straight for trouble!"

Nancy nodded but did not offer to turn back. Always fascinated by an intimation of something unknown or mysterious, she had, in the past, become involved in many exciting adventures. Friends often declared that she was good at finding the key to a baffling enigma partly because she was a "chip off the old block," referring to her brilliant father.

Nancy was quick to share the credit for her successes with her friends. Now, as she rang the bell of the Struthers residence, Nancy was glad that George was along. She could participate in what the young sleuth sensed was to be an unusual assignment.

"How nice to see you again, Nancy," Mrs. Struthers greeted her, as she opened the wide door. "And this must be the friend of whom you spoke. Come right in."

Introductions were acknowledged and the hostess led the girls into a tastefully decorated living room. Several bowls of flowers were attractively arranged, and a silver tea service had been set out on a low, carved antique table.

Although eager to hear about the mystery Mrs. Struthers had mentioned the evening before, Nancy restrained herself from bringing up the subject. "We met your granddaughter outside," she said. "Rose mentioned something about your dolls. Do you have a collection?"

"Does she!" cried Rose, who popped in the door. "Jiminy crickets, there are hundreds of dolls!"

"Rose, dear, don't shout so," Mrs. Struthers remonstrated quietly.

She turned to Nancy and George and told them that collecting dolls had been her hobby for the past few years. She had acquired them from nearly every country in the world.

"Perhaps you'd be interested in seeing them," she offered. "There's a great deal to be learned from dolls, even after we have given them up as playthings."

"Why is that?" inquired George, who had seldom played with dolls.

As Mrs. Struthers led the way down a long hall, she explained, "One can learn about people of long ago and about other countries from dolls."

Nancy caught her breath as the woman pushed a door open. Straight ahead against one wall of a large room was a tremendous rosewood cabinet with glass windows. On the shelves was Mrs. Struthers' collection.

"How lovely!" Nancy exclaimed. "You must have some real treasures here!"

Mrs. Struthers reached into the cabinet and selected a little old lady dressed in a red cape and black silk bonnet. Over her arm was a tiny basket.

"I have been fortunate in getting some unusual dolls," she told her guests. "This is one of the original peddlar dolls made in London in the nineteenth century. Notice the contents of her basket. '

The girls were fascinated to see so many miniature objects, including musical instruments, ribbons, and laces.

"Oh look!" George marveled. "There are even little pots and pans!"

"Imagine making something like this!" Nancy interjected. She reached into the basket and picked out a tiny set of knitting needles holding a half-completed miniature sock.

Just then the girls' attention was diverted by the sound of a tinkling melody. Rose motioned toward a small table where a beautiful doll stood on the velvet-covered box from which the music was coming.

"Watch!" she directed.

The doll began to move her head from side to side in time with the music. To add to her charm, she brought up one hand to smell a wee bouquet of flowers she was holding, while with the other she demurely waved a tiny, jeweled fan.

"She's darling," Nancy said.

Mrs. Struthers was delighted by her visitors' reaction, but suggested they return to the living room and have tea.

"Not for me," Rose sang out and left them.

"I'm afraid I have very little control over my lively granddaughter," the hostess lamented as she poured the tea. "Perhaps it's because she does not have the strong hand of a father.

"I feel I can tell you girls about this without fear of your violating my confidence," she went on. "Rose's father was a Spanish gypsy and a talented violinist. He gave many concerts in this country. My daughter became entranced with him and his exquisite playing. Against Mr. Struthers' and my wishes she left home to marry him."

Nancy now understood the reason for the woman's tears at the recital. "It must have been a great shock to you," she said.

Mrs. Struthers nodded. "We were very upset by my daughter's act and, I regret to say, rather harsh with her. She was banished from the family. When Rose was eight years old her father deserted them, and we pleaded with Enid to come home with her child."

"Did they?" George asked eagerly.

"Yes, but too late. My daughter was in poor health and heartbroken besides. Within a few months she died. Three months later, my dear husband passed away."

"I'm so sorry," Nancy said sympathetically.

"Rose is now my problem," the woman confessed. "She is not aware of her background, for her parents did not live with the tribe and never told her. Naturally, I never have breathed the truth.

"My granddaughter is very headstrong. She doesn't study in school, and runs off whenever it suits her fancy. If I leave her with adults or other children, she disgraces me by the things she says and does."

"Perhaps if you took Rose away for a year," Nancy suggested, but Mrs. Struthers shook her head.

"We did travel abroad for many months, but that only seemed to arouse wanderlust and a desire for freedom in her. Personally I enjoy traveling, and it gives me an opportunity to collect dolls. This means a great deal to me. I have been searching for one particular doll. Now I must stop, but I want you to continue the search. You will be given money to do it. I shall not be satisfied until I find the doll."

"Is it a rare one?" Nancy asked, intrigued by the assignment.

"Yes, the doll is connected with Rose's past. If I tell you my secret, you must never repeat it to her."

Nancy and George said they would respect the woman's wishes.

"When my beloved daughter lay on her deathbed, she talked half-deliriously about a doll. Almost her last words were, 'The doll! It's gone! Oh, Mother, you must find it for Rose.'"

"What did she mean?" George asked.

"I tried to find out, but Enid was too ill. I thought she said, 'Important. Very important. Clue—'"

At this instant a piercing shriek filled the air. Nancy was on her feet immediately and ran outside in the direction of the sound. George and Mrs. Struthers followed.

A car was driving away from the house with Rose half in, half out, of one of the open back doors. She was struggling with a woman.

CHAPTER III

Nancy's Assignment

"NANCY!" George cried. "Mrs. Struthers has fainted!"

"Take care of her," Nancy directed. "I'm going after Rose."

The young detective dashed to her car and hopped inside. Before she could start the motor, Rose had fallen to the side of the road. Nancy jumped out of the vehicle and raced to her.

"Are you hurt?" she asked anxiously, picking Rose up. "What happened?"

The girl clutched Nancy tightly and seemed more frightened than harmed. "I'm—all—right, I guess, but I don't ever w-want to see those aw-awful people again." She sobbed hysterically.

Nancy realized that the child was so over-wrought that it would be hard to get a clear account from her of what had happened. "Had you ever seen them before?" she asked.

"N-no, they just stopped in front of the house and asked about Gran's d-dolls. I told them to come in, but they said no, we had callers."

"Then what happened?"

"The woman said it would be better if I brought out one of the rare dolls, so I d-did. When I held it up to show her, she grabbed it. I tried to get it back, but just then the man started the car, and I was half in it!" She shuddered.

"There, there, Rose, you're all right now," Nancy soothed her, "although you did have quite a fall. Try to describe the people."

"They were real mean-looking, and the woman had funny red hair. I never thought they'd steal Gran's doll."

"Which doll was it?" Nancy asked.

"The one on the music box, holding the fan," Rose said, as Nancy led her back to the house.

Mrs. Struthers had revived and was relieved that her granddaughter was safe. "Oh, my dear child!" she exclaimed and hugged Rose. "Are you all right?"

"I'll be okay in a jiff, Gran," Rose told her, wriggling out of the embrace.

"What happened?" Mrs. Struthers asked. After Nancy had related Rose's story, the woman said, "Thank goodness you girls were here."

Although Mrs. Struthers was concerned over losing one of her precious dolls, she protested when Nancy suggested notifying the police. "I wish to avoid publicity. I'd prefer having you help me, Nancy. If you'll come tomorrow, I'll tell you the rest of my story."

By this time, Nancy was more intrigued than ever with the case. "I'll be here," she promised.

At dinner that evening, Nancy told her father about the happenings of the afternoon. "The thieves got away in a black sedan," she said regretfully, "and the license plate was so smeared with mud I couldn't read it. But I did notice that the car was a new model."

"A slim clue," Carson Drew observed.

"I've promised to help Mrs. Struthers." Nancy smiled. "Rose needs help too. She's rude and undisciplined, but I think with her musical heritage she'd improve under some sort of artistic training."

"I'm afraid it will take a good bit of training," Mr. Drew declared.

The next day Nancy was about to leave for Mrs. Struthers' home when her friend Bess Marvin arrived. Attractive and slightly plump, Bess was as feminine as George Fayne, her cousin, was tomboyish. Bess was eager to go on a shopping spree. "Grab your pocketbook and we'll be off!"

Nancy shook her head. "Sorry, Bess, I can't make it."

"You're going somewhere with Ned Nickerson." Bess teased.

"No."

"Then you're working on another mystery."

"Yes." Nancy smiled. "Hop in the car and I'll drop you off at the mall." On the way Nancy brought Bess up-to-date on her new case.

"How I'd love to see those dolls!" Bess sighed when the girls arrived at the shopping center.

Nancy promised to take her to the Struthers' home soon. In a few minutes the young detective was seated in the doll collector's living room. Mrs. Struthers explained that Rose was visiting a neighbor so there would be no interruptions.

"You missed the most important part of my story yesterday," the woman began in a quiet voice. "I was telling you my daughter's dying words."

"Yes, said Nancy. "You mentioned something about a clue."

"A clue I've tried unsuccessfully to find," Mrs. Struthers confided, "though I think it may be here. Perhaps you can uncover it."

She unlocked a cabinet and removed a thick book. It appeared to be an old family album, covered with brass filigree work and studded with precious stones of various colors.

"This is a very valuable possession," the woman explained, "and is filled with family photographs."

"How does it tie in with the clue?" Nancy asked.

Mrs. Struthers sighed. "As my daughter lay on

her deathbed, she seemed worried about Rose's future. She tried desperately to tell me something. Her last words were, 'Clue in . . . the old album.' "

"In this one, you think?" Nancy queried as she turned the pages of the photograph album.

"I'm not sure," Mrs. Struthers replied. Nancy stopped to look at the picture of a pretty child of about eight years of age. She was holding a doll. "That one is my daughter, Enid, when she was a little girl," the woman said. "And here is a picture of Enid in her wedding dress."

"Your daughter was beautiful," said Nancy. "And the dress is lovely."

"I never saw it." Mrs. Struthers sighed. "Enid bought the dress herself and later, when she needed money, she sold it. When she returned home, she slipped this picture into the album. I found it after her death."

"What was her married name?"

"Pepito. Mrs. Romano Pepito. But Rose uses the name of Struthers."

"Your daughter's final words were, 'The doll. It's gone. Find it for Rose,' " Nancy said. "Could she have meant the doll she holds in the photograph of herself as a child?"

"I thought so at first, but that doll is here in the house. It gave me no clue."

"Apparently the lost doll holds a secret to

something that would mean a great deal to Rose."
Nancy mused.

"Exactly," the grandmother agreed. "Rose may
have a hidden fortune somewhere."

"You've searched the old album thoroughly?"

"Dozens of times. But perhaps your young eyes
might detect something I've missed."

Nancy was eager to examine the album.

"It's possible my daughter didn't mean this album," Mrs. Struthers remarked thoughtfully.
"She may have intended to tell me the all-im-
portant clue was hidden in an album belonging to
the Pepito family."

"Have you talked to any of them about it?"

"Impossible. I have no idea where they are
living."

"Can Rose explain what her mother meant?"

"She knew almost nothing about the Pepitos.
My daughter was careful to keep such information
from her. Enid told me very little. While she was
here she scarcely mentioned her husband's name,
although I know Enid thought of him constantly."

During the next hour, Nancy carefully went
through the album. She could find no clue that
appeared to have any bearing on the mystery.

"If we only had some hint about the doll your
daughter meant," Nancy said. "Even knowing if
it had been misplaced, or perhaps sold, would
help."

"I rather doubt either of those possibilities," Mrs. Struthers replied.

"It may have been stolen," Nancy ventured.

The elderly woman hesitated. "There is something rather ominous that may be connected with the doll's disappearance," she confessed. "The jeweled album contained a note written in a strange handwriting. I was afraid Rose might see it some day and ask questions, so I destroyed it."

"What did the paper say?"

"I can never forget the words," Mrs. Struthers replied. " 'The source of light will heal all ills, but a curse will follow him who takes it from the gypsies!' "

"What a strange message!" Nancy exclaimed.

"My daughter must have placed the note in the jeweled album," Mrs. Struthers explained, "although her reason for doing it puzzles me."

"It may be a good clue," declared Nancy. "Perhaps a member of her husband's tribe sent the note."

"Quite likely. I have always thought the writer meant it as a warning—perhaps to frighten my daughter."

"True," Nancy said. "Or even a friendly warning."

"What do you think the message meant?" Mrs. Struthers asked.

Nancy shrugged. "Perhaps that the doll, which

may light up or be adorned with shiny jewels, would bring bad luck to any owner but a gypsy."

"In that case, maybe you had better not search for it," said Mrs. Struthers, alarmed. "I should not want any harm to come to you."

Nancy smiled. "Please don't worry. I'll be careful. The mystery is too intriguing to drop now."

"If you do find the doll, I'll see that you are properly compensated," the collector told her.

"My reward will be the fun I'll have searching for the doll," Nancy said.

"And perhaps in adding it to my collection," Mrs. Struthers suggested.

"I think I'd better see what dolls you have, so I won't duplicate them."

During the next hour and a half Nancy inspected the figures in the cabinet. The task took longer than she had expected, for they were so fascinating she could not bring herself to pass over them lightly.

The variety of materials the dolls were made of amazed the girl. Some were fashioned from such substances as cornhusks, dried apples, and horsehair. One was just the bust of a lovely Asiatic lady.

"It's a Chinese head doll," Mrs. Struthers explained, "made of unglazed ceramic called *bisque*. In the mid-nineteenth century, china heads and limbs were made to go on wooden bodies. Now this little lady," she added, picking up one in a quaint evening dress, "is Jenny Lind, the famous singer. You know, she first appeared in this country under the sponsorship of P.T. Barnum, of circus fame."

"I see now that a person can learn a lot about history by collecting dolls. Where does the word 'doll' come from?"

"The origin of the word isn't clear, though many authorities believe it's a contraction of the English name Dorothy. In old Saxon times there was a word *dol*, meaning figure, and the Greeks used the word *ei-DOL-on*, which meant idol."

"One can even learn about a language from dolls," Nancy remarked, her eyes twinkling.

The girl's gaze roved to a French swordsman high in the cabinet. The stalwart fellow stood alertly on guard, with his tiny steel saber poised as if to duel an imaginary opponent.

"How tricky!" Nancy exclaimed.

As she removed the figure from its niche, something sharp pierced her finger. The prick was deep and made Nancy wince.

"Why, the sword doll wounded me!" She laughed, rubbing her finger.

Mrs. Struthers was amazed, for she had never noticed that the sword was so sharp. Blood oozed from Nancy's finger.

"I'll get you a bandage," the woman offered.

"Please don't bother. The prick is nothing." Nancy wrapped a tissue around her finger and gingerly put the sword doll back on the shelf.

Just then an outside door slammed. A moment later Rose stomped angrily into the room.

"Home early, aren't you, dear?" her grandmother observed.

"Yes, and I'll never play with that horrid girl again! She said I'm bossy and wild."

"Oh, Rose, why can't you behave like a little lady and get along with your playmates?" Mrs. Struthers fretted.

" 'Cause I'm not a lady yet and anyway maybe I don't want to be one! Maybe I'll be—I might even be a gypsy!"

"Don't say that!" Mrs. Struthers scolded.

To relieve the tension Nancy changed the subject by asking Rose again about the man and woman who had stolen the doll the previous day. Rose told her that the man had dark eyes and hair, and a scar on his forehead. The woman had carrot-colored hair.

Nancy began to feel dizzy. She brushed a hand across her eyes. Everything in the room seemed blurred. As if from far away, she heard Rose cry out, "Granny, look at Nancy! She's white as a ghost!"

"I feel strange," Nancy mumbled.

Mrs. Struthers grasped the girl's arm and

guided her to a couch. Nancy collapsed upon it.

"What's the matter with her?" Rose asked, terror-stricken.

"I don't know. She was all right a moment ago. I can't understand it."

Nancy, fighting the dizziness, thought she knew what had happened. "Send . . . for a . . . doctor," she pleaded. "I think . . . the sword doll . . poisoned . . . me!"

Then she lapsed into unconsciousness.

CHAPTER IV

The Child Bride

MRS. STRUTHERS became hysterical at Nancy's sudden collapse. Mrs. Carroll, the housekeeper, hurried into the room.

"Nancy's been poisoned!" Mrs. Struthers exclaimed. "Call Mr. Drew and Dr. Burney at once!"

Mrs. Carroll rushed to the telephone and summoned the two men, who reached the Struthers' home at the same time. Mrs. Struthers explained what had happened.

"There's the doll that pricked Nancy. She thought it poisoned her. Oh, this dreadful thing is all my fault!"

Dr. Burney examined Nancy. "She has been poisoned all right," he announced. "The dose probably was a light one, and she'll be all right. I'd like to find out what it was, though, so I can give her an antidote."

Mr. Drew examined the sword doll. It took him a few minutes before he found a tiny button at the hilt of the sword. When he pressed it, a needle shot out. From it dripped a single drop of fluid.

"How dreadful!" Mrs. Struthers cried.

Dr. Burney identified the poison by its odor and prepared an antidote. "Your daughter will probably sleep heavily for an hour," he told the lawyer, "and should be kept quiet until tomorrow."

Mr. Drew wanted to take Nancy home, but the physician advised against this. Mrs. Struthers insisted that the young girl remain where she was. Mr. Drew suggested that it might be helpful if Hannah Gruen stayed with Nancy for the night.

Mrs. Struthers agreed to the plan, and within half an hour Mrs. Gruen arrived in a taxi. She listened to the doctor's orders and promised they would be carried out to the letter.

"Call me if Nancy fails to awaken within an hour," the physician instructed as he was leaving.

When almost an hour had elapsed and she had not awakened, Mr. Drew became alarmed. As he was about to call the doctor, Nancy opened her eyes. "Where am I?" she mumbled, sitting up.

"With Hannah and me," said Mr. Drew. He placed his daughter back gently against the pillow. "Everything is all right."

Reassured, Nancy sighed and snuggled down for some more sleep. Mr. Drew was satisfied that she was out of danger and left.

The next morning Mrs. Struthers brought in the River Heights *Gazette* from the porch. She gasped as she read the headline.

NANCY DREW POISONED BY MYSTERIOUS
DOLL AT STRUTHERS HOME

"Good gracious!" the woman exclaimed. "Where did the paper ever learn about this?"

She was sure no one in the house had given the story to the newspaper. As her mind flew from one possibility to another, she stopped short in her thinking.

Rose!

Mrs. Struthers recalled that her granddaughter had been away from the house after Nancy's accident the previous afternoon. As soon as Rose appeared, Mrs. Struthers showed her the headline.

"Rose, what do you know about this?"

"Oh, I told some kids down the street, and Lorna's father writes for the paper."

"This article even describes how that couple in the car stole our fan doll, and I didn't want any publicity about it!"

"I mentioned that when he called to confirm the story."

Mrs. Struthers sighed. "Whatever shall I do with you, Rose?"

The girl became sulky and would not eat breakfast. The situation was not relieved when Nancy appeared and saw the newspaper account. She had recovered from the effects of the poison, but this new development embarrassed and disturbed her.

When Nancy and Hannah reached home, they were besieged with phone calls from interested friends. Ned Nickerson, a special college friend of Nancy's, suggested they attend a carnival that evening to get Nancy's mind off the situation.

At seven o'clock handsome, dark-haired Ned arrived. He was working this summer as counselor at a boys' camp. The couple drove to Claymore and enjoyed the carnival with its gay crowds and many amusements. They stopped first at a shooting gallery, where Ned won a large stuffed animal, which he presented to Nancy.

"What shall we do next?" he asked. "Want to try the ferris wheel?"

Nancy shook her head. "Listen!" she exclaimed.

"To what? That gypsy's fiddle?"

"Are there gypsies in this carnival?"

"Sure, down at the far end. They have several fortunetelling tents. Want to have a reading?"

"Let's!"

"Not me." Ned laughed. "My future is pretty well set, and I don't want anyone tampering with it. I'll go into business, prosper, and marry a certain ambitious young lady named. . . ."

"Come on, Ned," Nancy broke in. "I'm not so much interested in fortunes myself, but I do want to hear that violinist play. A case I'm working on has something to do with a gypsy violinist."

They hastened to the tents, where a cluster of bright-eyed, bronze-skinned children stared at them. A woman in a colorful red and yellow skirt hurriedly took up her post in front of one of the tents. Her flashing eyes studied Nancy.

"Cross my palm with money and I will tell your fortune, pretty miss," she said.

Nancy shook her head, for she was listening intently to a violin solo.

"Isn't that the *Hungarian Rhapsody?*" Nancy murmured to Ned. "Maybe the violinist is Romano!"

"Who's he?" Ned asked. "A rival of mine?"

Nancy did not explain, for she noticed that the woman was listening attentively to every word she and Ned were saying. Her gaze was so penetrating that the girl felt ill at ease.

"May we speak to the violinist?" Nancy asked her.

"No, it is not allowed," the woman replied.

She turned and whispered to a couple of children. One of the youngsters scurried away from the tent, and a moment later the violin playing ended abruptly.

"At least tell us the name of your gifted musician," Nancy urged. The woman shrugged her shoulders and went into the tent.

"Nice, sociable people!" Ned commented.

He and Nancy wandered on and tried to catch a glimpse of the violinist. Evidently the child had warned him and he had fled.

As the couple walked along the row of tents, they were scrutinized by everyone around. No one again offered to tell Nancy's fortune. When a little boy came to Ned and begged for money, his mother spoke sharply to him. The child scampered off without taking the coin Ned offered him.

"What's the matter with everybody?" he asked, puzzled. "It's as if they're afraid we'll find out something they want to keep secret!"

The longer Nancy and Ned stayed, the more tense the atmosphere became, so finally they left and returned to the main section of the carnival. There they asked one of the concessionaires where the gypsies had come from.

"Spain, I believe," the man replied. "Guess they're fixing to leave the carnival a few days after the wedding."

"What wedding?" Nancy inquired.

"Why, the one tonight at ten o'clock. Didn't you see the sign? They're marrying off a child bride."

"No, we didn't," Nancy said. "I'd love to go to the ceremony. But I thought gypsy weddings were for gypsies only."

"They usually are," the man agreed. "This one would have been too, only the carnival manager got their chief, Zorus, to agree to let the public attend."

"For a fee, no doubt," Ned added.

"Oh, sure, a high one at that. But it's only tonight that outsiders can go. A gypsy wedding sometimes goes on for six or seven days, with dancing and feasting."

"Where can we get tickets?" Ned asked.

"At the first tent from here. I've been told it won't be worth the price, though. All that happens is the chief speaks a few words, and they give the child bride a doll. Then the dancing begins. That's the best part."

Nancy's eyes kindled at mention of a ceremony involving a doll. She might pick up a clue. Then her eager expression turned to one of dismay.

"Ned," she said, "maybe the gypsies won't let us in!"

"We'll soon find out," he replied.

The two purposely stayed away from the gypsy section of the carnival until nearly ten o'clock. Then Nancy said, "If we go in separately, maybe they won't spot us."

She was right. Eager last-minute attendants at the performance jostled them and they were not noticed by the ticket seller or any other gypsies.

Music for the wedding was furnished by three handsome young fiddlers. Nancy liked their gay, colorful costumes. Because of the men's ages she knew none of them could be Rose's father. After listening to the music, she also concluded that not one of the musicians had the fine touch of the violinist who had played the *Hungarian Rhapsody* a little while before.

"That other violinist could have been Romano Pepito," Nancy thought. "Oh, how I wish I might see him!"

At this moment the musicians changed to another melody, soft and sweet. From a tent stepped a middle-aged man wearing a red-and-yellow suit and long, round earrings. He was the master of ceremonies and walked to the center of the ring.

"According to gypsy custom," he said to the audience, "the price for the bride must be paid before the wedding takes place. In olden days horses were given, but now we prefer money."

The gaudily attired young bridegroom and the father of the bride came forward. The former took a small pouch of jingling coins from a pocket and handed it to the other, who thanked him. Then the three fiddlers struck up a solemn march.

"Oh, this must be the chief," Nancy concluded, as a tall, elderly man in a long, embroidered red robe stalked from another tent. Piercing black eyes looked out above a heavy, iron-gray beard. He spoke to the other men, then the bride's father went into a tent.

"We are true gypsies," the master of ceremonies explained, "and our girls marry very young. But we have complied with all the laws of this state. Our leader, Zorus, will now unite Melchor and Luisa in a Romany wedding ceremony."

The musicians began to play a livelier air, but this did not help to calm the bride as she stepped nervously from her tent. Nancy's heart went out to the beautiful young girl, who looked very frightened and could not have been more than fourteen years old. She was dressed in an embroidered white silk gown, which had become yellowed with age.

The ceremony was performed by Zorus in the space of a few minutes. Nancy studied his cruel face. "I wouldn't trust him," she thought.

A loaf of bread, salt, and a bottle of wine were brought out as symbols of plenty. Zorus broke the bread and sprinkled salt on each half. The bride and groom exchanged halves, each taking a bite and a sip of wine.

Zorus now motioned to the announcer, who said, "It has been a custom for hundreds of years, at weddings of our tribe, to present the child bride with a doll. Today our bride is not exactly a child, but we shall follow that custom."

Nancy watched intently as an elderly gypsy woman walked forward with a basket. Possibly Rose's father at the time of his marriage had given his bride a gypsy doll. It might have been a duplicate of the one about to be presented!

"If it was and that's the one I'm to look for, I may be a long way toward solving Mrs. Struthers' mystery," she concluded.

When the gift was held up, Nancy's hopes fell. It was only an inexpensive factory-made doll, and so new it could have no significance for her.

In a few moments the violinists began to play dance music, and the crowd milled around. Ned found Nancy and asked if she had enjoyed the ceremony.

"Oh, yes," she replied. "For just a second I thought I had found a good clue, but nothing came of it. Let's watch the performance a few minutes longer and then go home."

Though the tribal dances were interesting to watch, Nancy found her gaze wandering toward a middle-aged gypsy couple who stood off to one side.

"That man and woman look familiar to me," the girl thought. "And yet I don't know any gypsies."

She noticed that they were staring at her, but when she faced them directly they looked away and edged toward the exit.

"Why did they do that?" Nancy wondered.

Suddenly she believed she knew who they were. The man had a scar on his forehead. The woman had carrot-red hair. They fitted Rose's description of the couple who had stolen Mrs. Struthers' fan doll!

CHAPTER V

Foiled

NANCY grabbed Ned's arm and hurried after the suspects. An old woman stopped the gypsy couple and addressed the man as Anton and the woman as Nitaka.

"I think they might be the thieves who came to Mrs. Struthers' in a black sedan!" Nancy whispered to Ned. "If so, their car must be parked on the grounds and there might be some evidence in it. Want to see if you can find it?"

"Sure thing. What's the license number?"

"I don't know, Ned. But look for a new black sedan. I'll wait here for you. I want to watch Anton and Nitaka."

Ned slipped away quietly and Nancy followed the gypsy couple. Presently they stopped and she sauntered up to them and asked a question about the wedding ceremony. Anton gazed at her with hostile eyes and made a brief reply.

Nancy then brought up the subject of dolls. Instead of talking to her, Anton said something to Nitaka in the Romany language. The couple turned their backs and walked away.

A few minutes later Nancy spotted them talking confidentially to Zorus. As they left him, she caught the word "Drew." They must be talking about her!

Ned returned to report he had found not one but three black sedans that would answer Nancy's description. He also handed her a scrap of soiled paper.

"Found this on the ground near one of the cars," he explained. "It's a receipt that may interest you."

The paper read, "For one doll, $100—" The rest had been torn off, and the names of both buyer and seller were missing.

"This certainly does interest me!" Nancy cried. "We must find the other part of the paper. Show me where you picked this up."

Ned led her to the dimly lighted parking lot. "The note was lying on the ground by this black sedan," he pointed out. "There was no other paper anywhere around."

"This car looks like the one that stopped at the Struthers'," Nancy said. "Maybe if we wait, we'll see who the owner is. And if he should turn out to be Anton or Nitaka. . . ."

"Hey, not so fast." Ned laughed.

"We must find the other part of the paper," Nancy said.

He and Nancy searched the ground for the missing part of the receipt but did not find it. Presently they heard someone coming.

"It may be Anton or Nitaka!" Nancy whispered.

They slipped behind another parked car and saw a young man walk over to the sedan and unlock the door. Ned came out of hiding.

"Just a minute, sir," he said. "May we ask you a few questions?"

Startled, the fellow whirled around. Then Ned burst into laughter.

"Bill Jones!" he exclaimed, recognizing a college friend whom Nancy also knew.

"From the way you spoke, I take it you thought I was a crook!" Bill grinned after he had greeted Nancy and her escort.

"Something like that," Ned admitted. "Is this your car?"

"It will be when I finish the payments on it. What are you and Nancy doing here? Sleuthing?"

"We came to see the carnival," Nancy explained, "but now we're looking for some thieves."

"Sorry I can't oblige you," Bill teased. "Want a lift to River Heights?"

"No, thanks, Bill, we have a car," Ned replied.

He and Nancy waited for the owners of the other black sedans, but did not see Anton, Nitaka, or any other gypsies.

"Well, I failed on all my clues tonight," Nancy said as she and Ned walked to their car. "Or did I? Maybe learning who those suspects are will be worthwhile."

Nancy's exciting visit to the carnival did not prevent her from sleeping soundly. At breakfast she said to her father, "Dad, have you a date to-night?"

"No. Why do you ask?"

"Will you go somewhere with me?"

"With you?" Mr. Drew replied, chuckling. "I'd be delighted."

"Maybe you won't be so pleased when you hear where it is. I'd like to take Rose to the carnival."

"Oh, no!"

"Only to have her look at Anton and Nitaka to see if they're the ones who stole the fan doll."

"That's different," said Mr. Drew. "All right."

Mrs. Struthers consented to the plan, and Rose was thrilled. When she and the Drews reached the fairgrounds, she insisted on trying all the rides. Nancy joined her on a few but soon begged to stay on the sidelines with her father.

The carnival manager passed by as Rose was on The Whip. Nancy asked him where the gypsies had gone. To her disappointment he said the group had moved out early that morning.

"That old fellow Zorus was a strange guy," the manager remarked. "Never even said they were leaving."

"How about Anton and Nitaka?" Nancy queried. "Did they go with the others?"

"I didn't know any of them except their king."

"King?" Mr. Drew inquired. "Was Zorus their king?"

"That's what they called him," the manager explained. "And treated him like one, too."

On the drive home Rose fell asleep in the back seat. Nancy reflected on the information she had received from the carnival manager. Were the couple she suspected of stealing Mrs. Struthers' doll subjects of Zorus? Had he, perhaps, instructed Anton and Nitaka to take it?

Mr. Drew broke in on his daughter's thoughts. "Guess you scared the gypsies away," he said.

"I'll keep on looking for Anton and Nitaka just the same," Nancy replied.

When the Drews delivered Rose to her home, Mrs. Struthers requested that Nancy attend a sale of dolls in another state the following week. She suggested that George and Bess go with her. Nancy agreed.

At nine o'clock Monday morning, she and her friends met at the River Heights airport and boarded a plane for Jefferson. When the girls were seated and ready for takeoff a last-minute passenger rushed inside. She flopped into an aisle seat several rows ahead of Nancy, Bess, and George.

Nancy nudged her friends. "Nitaka just got on the plane!" she whispered.

"You mean that carrot-haired woman?" Bess asked. "She isn't wearing gypsy clothes."

"The woman who stole Mrs. Struthers' doll wasn't wearing them at the time, either," said Nancy. "The gypsies left the carnival, but evidently they didn't move very far away," she guessed.

"Where do you suppose Nitaka's going?" George asked.

"I have no idea, but I mean to follow her, now that I have a chance," Nancy decided. "If she doesn't get off at Jefferson, I'll stay on the plane until she does."

"Oh, please don't," Bess begged. "You might get into trouble!"

"What about the doll sale?" George asked.

"You girls will have to go to it." As the cousins groaned and insisted they could not do the job without her, Nancy replied, "If Nitaka is a thief and she could lead me to something important, you wouldn't want me to give up the chase, would you?"

"I suppose not," George said grudgingly.

Not once during the flight to Jefferson did Nitaka glance over her shoulder. She seemed indifferent to the scenery and devoted herself to a booklet, which she read many times.

The girls were the first passengers off the plane when it landed at Jefferson. They kept out of sight and watched to see if Nitaka would alight also.

Nancy had just about decided she was not going to, when the woman appeared. She hastened through the terminal and jumped into a cab.

"Hurry, or we'll lose her!" Nancy cried out to her friends.

After a little delay the girls found a taxi. By this time Nitaka's cab was far down the road.

"Will you please try to overtake that taxi?" Nancy asked their driver.

The elderly man was not willing to do so. As they reached the heart of Jefferson, they realized they had lost the trail of the other vehicle.

"It turned down a side street somewheres," the driver mumbled. "I was watching sharp, but I didn't see which way it went."

"Never mind." Nancy sighed. "Please drive us to the Jefferson Galleries."

It was now after eleven and Nancy feared many of the dolls might have been sold.

"We'll have to hurry or we'll be too late," she declared. "I hope I haven't failed Mrs. Struthers."

Ten minutes later the girls were at the galleries. The salesrooms were thronged with customers. Nancy was relieved to learn that while nearly all the fine old silver and jewelry had been sold, few of the dolls had been.

"Why did Mrs. Struthers want you to come to this particular sale?" Bess asked as the girls walked toward the counter where the dolls were displayed.

"Most of the dolls are old and valuable, so there's a chance the stolen fan doll is here, and even the one Mrs. Struthers' daughter wanted her to find," Nancy explained.

She examined the dolls carefully, but found none that she wanted. Nancy asked a salesman if he had any others for sale that were not on display —any that lighted up or had gems sewed on their costumes.

"The most attractive dolls have been sold," he answered. "One like the one you mention was among them. A king with a jeweled robe."

"Just my luck!" Nancy groaned. "Who bought the doll?"

"The woman didn't give her name. She paid cash. Oh, there she is—leaving with her package."

Nancy turned and caught a glimpse of the retreating figure who was now outside the galleries. Nitaka!

Nancy ran after the gypsy, but was too late to stop her. Nitaka entered a taxi and already was far down the street before the girl reached the sidewalk.

"This is the worst yet!" Nancy said when she returned to Bess and George. "That woman may have bought the very doll I'm trying to find!"

The manager overheard Nancy's remark. He introduced himself and said, "If you're interested in fine dolls, perhaps you'd like to see one that is more valuable than any sold here today."

"Is it for sale?" Nancy asked, hope reviving in her.

"No, and we never have displayed the doll. Wait here and I'll bring it from the back room."

The manager was gone at least ten minutes. When he returned, the girls saw at once that something was wrong.

"What became of that doll we kept in the office safe?" he asked several salesmen.

"You removed it this morning," one of the men reminded him.

"Yes, one of the doll's hands needed repairing. I took it out of the safe and put it on my desk. Now it's gone! Someone must have sold it by mistake!"

Each of the salesmen denied taking part in such a transaction.

"Then the doll has been stolen!" the manager cried. "In the hands of the wrong person, it can be a very dangerous thing!"

CHAPTER VI

Upsetting News

NANCY asked the manager of the Jefferson Galleries what he meant about the doll's being dangerous, but he was reluctant to tell her.

"Is the doll one of the poisonous types?" she asked.

The man gave her a startled glance. "Why . . . er . . . yes. It is," he admitted nervously. "We intended to sell the witch doll to a museum, and therefore hadn't removed the poisonous powder from it. When you touch a certain spot, the powder sifts out. Its fumes induce deep sleep. An overdose could be fatal!"

"Oh!" Bess cried.

"You'll notify the police and the newspapers at once?" Nancy suggested. "If the information is published, the thief or anyone else will be warned before he's harmed."

"Yes. I'll call them right now," the manager

promised. As he started away, he mumbled something about how it would serve the thief right if he were poisoned.

The girls were about to leave the galleries when Nancy noticed a half-opened chest filled with dolls. A salesman came toward her and asked if she were interested.

"There are some unusual items in this chest," he said. "Here's one that may interest you," he added, offering Nancy a strange-looking figure with four different faces. "It dates back to about 1870."

One side of the bisque head laughed, one cried, another pouted, and the fourth had its eyes closed as if in sleep. The head rotated in a socket so that a child playing with the doll could choose whatever expression she desired.

"How much is this one?" Nancy asked. She felt sure Mrs. Struthers would like to add it to her collection.

The man mentioned a price below what Nancy had expected, so she quickly made the purchase. While the young girl waited for the package to be wrapped, her gaze fastened on a counter stacked with albums. Eagerly she looked among the old plush-covered books. Several were family albums decorated with raised, ornate words.

"Albums like those aren't unusual," George said impatiently. "My grandmother has a couple of them. Please come!"

But Nancy continued to look through the stack of albums. Then a name on one at the bottom of the pile caught her eye.

Euphemia Struthers

Eagerly Nancy flipped the pages, but was disappointed to find that every photograph had been removed. Nevertheless, hopeful that this Euphemia might have been related to Mrs. Struthers, and that the album might contain the clue Rose's mother had spoken of on her deathbed, Nancy purchased the book.

"Now, let's leave before you find something else to buy!" George pleaded, pulling Nancy away.

The girls lunched at a tearoom across the street. Later they went for a walk before returning to the airport.

As they passed an empty lot at the end of a dead-end street, Bess kicked aside a soiled and stained piece of paper. George picked it up.

"Looks like an old concert program," she said.

"That's exactly what it is," Nancy added as she read over George's shoulder. "And see whose name is featured—Romano Pepito's!"

"The gypsy violinist!" Bess exclaimed. "How did it get here?"

"From the looks of this lot a gypsy caravan could have camped here recently." Nancy explained. She walked over to a pile on the ground and discovered it was a tattered old tent. There were also the remains of a fire.

"Perhaps some of the campers knew Romano Pepito," Bess said.

"He may even have been here himself!" Nancy suggested. "Oh, I'd give anything to find the group and ask them about Pepito."

"No time to do that now," George said. "If we're going to catch the plane to River Heights, we'd better hop a cab to the airport."

The driver made such a quick trip to the terminal, that Nancy had time to call Mrs. Struthers and tell her about the purchases. Mrs. Carroll answered the phone.

"Oh, Nancy, something dreadful has happened since you've been gone. Can you come here direct from the plane?"

The young detective agreed to do that. When she reached the Struthers' home, the housekeeper was waiting for her.

"Matters are in a bad state," Mrs. Carroll said.

"What's wrong?"

"A child in the neighborhood, Janie Bond, started a story that Rose's father is a gypsy. To make it worse, she said all gypsies are thieves!"

"Oh, how unfair!" Nancy exclaimed. "Rose's father was a talented violinist."

"Yes, I know," the housekeeper agreed. "Mrs. Struthers told me the whole story this morning, but she hasn't mentioned a thing to Rose."

"Why not?"

"I don't know, and naturally Rose believes

what Janie says. Won't you see what you can do
with Mrs. Struthers?"

"Is she in her room?"

"Yes. She gets more beside herself by the minute. I wanted to call the doctor, but she wouldn't
let me."

Nancy hurried up the stairs and went direct to
Mrs. Struthers, who was lying on the bed.

"Oh, my dear, what am I going to do?" the
anxious woman cried out.

Nancy took Mrs. Struthers' hand in her own
and tried to quiet her. "Please don't be so upset,"
she said. "Children say things without thinking
and forget them the next minute."

"But not this," Mrs. Struthers said. "The dis-
grace of it! Things were bad enough before, but
now to have everyone think my daughter married
a thief!"

"Please, Mrs. Struthers. Intelligent people
know most gypsies are fine people, and wouldn't
believe little Janie Bond."

Nancy went on to say that what other people
thought was of far less importance anyway than
what the blow might do to Rose. "She's a sensitive
child, and if things aren't straightened out in her
mind she may do something drastic."

"In what way?" Mrs. Struthers asked.

"Oh, run away, for instance."

The woman looked frightened. She did not
speak for several seconds, then said, "Nancy, you

are a wise person. I can see I lost my head. I'll tell
Rose everything at once!"

As the woman rose from the bed Nancy laid a
restraining hand on her shoulder. "Would you
like to suggest to Rose that on account of her
father's work he was unable to return to his
family, but that he will as soon as he can?"

Mrs. Struthers smiled. "It is very good advice.
I'll take it. Will you come with me?"

"No. I'll wait in the living room."

Mrs. Struthers went to Rose's room and stayed
for half an hour. Then the two went downstairs,
where Nancy was waiting.

How changed both looked! They were actually
smiling at each other! Nancy learned that the
only barrier not crossed was that Rose stubbornly
refused to return to school. She was afraid children might make fun of her.

Again Mrs. Struthers appealed to Nancy, who
thought a moment, then said, "Why don't you ar-
range to have Rose tutored at home and add music
and dancing to her studies?"

"Oh, please let me, Granny," Rose pleaded.
"And I want to play the violin like my father!"

"All right," Mrs. Struthers agreed. "Whom do
you recommend, Nancy? I don't know any teachers in River Heights."

Nancy knew an excellent retired schoolteacher
and gave Mrs. Struthers her name and address. She
also wrote down those of the best music and danc-

ing teachers in River Heights. Mrs. Struthers thanked her profusely for the help.

As Nancy left the house, she decided to talk to Janie Bond. "How in the world did that girl learn Rose is part gypsy?"

At the school Nancy found out from some little girls who Janie was and stopped her as she started home. The child became frightened when she realized she was being questioned about Rose.

"I don't know anything about her," she said sullenly, "so let me go."

"Who told you Rose is a gypsy?"

"I'm not going to tell!"

"Then I'll ask your mother." Nancy walked off in the direction of the Bond home.

"No, wait!" Frantically Janie ran after her. "Don't tell Mom the story I started!" she pleaded. "I'll explain anything you want to know."

"I'm so glad you changed your mind, Janie," Nancy said. "First, tell me who told you Rose is a gypsy?"

"A strange woman," Janie explained. "I was in front of our school with some kids when she drove up. She asked us if Rose had come out yet."

"And you said?"

"That Rose had gone home."

"Did the woman look like a gypsy?"

Janie shrugged. "She was real dark and had red hair and wore big earrings. She asked us a lot of questions about Rose."

"What were they?"

"She wanted to know what time Rose came to school and what time she went home. Then she told us Rose's father was a gypsy. That's all."

"But that's not all. You told other children."

"I made up the rest," Janie admitted. "I'm sorry. Honestly I am."

"Rose is the daughter of a great violinist," Nancy told the girl. "I've heard too that he's a Spanish gypsy, but that's not to his discredit. Most gypsies are fine people. Some are excellent musicians and a few are movie stars."

Janie felt ashamed and wanted to leave. Nancy said, "Tell me more about the mysterious woman who said Rose's father was a gypsy. Did the lady drive up in a black sedan?"

"Yes, and she got real mad when Billy West upset her suitcase."

"Suitcase?"

"She had a little one in her hand when she got out of the car. Billy pushed against the bag and it opened. Guess what she had inside?"

"You tell me."

"Dolls! I thought she must sell them, only they didn't look new. The kids all wanted to see them, but the woman was real cross. She closed the suitcase with a bang."

"Did you see the dolls yourself, Janie?"

"Sure, I was standing right there all the time."

"What were they like?" Nancy asked, excited.

"Oh, they weren't like the dolls in the stores. One had a fan in her hand. Another was a little man playing a violin."

Janie's information convinced Nancy that the woman was the person who had stolen Mrs. Struthers' fan doll. The description Janie had given fitted Nitaka!

"Did the doll with the fan stand on a velvet box?" Nancy inquired.

"I think so," Janie recalled. "The woman slammed the suitcase shut so fast we didn't get a very good look at the dolls. Billy asked her if she sold them. She said yes. Then she jumped in her car and drove away."

Nancy's suspicions were confirmed. She was certain that the woman with the dolls was Nitaka and that a plot was afoot to harm Rose.

"May I go now?" Janie asked impatiently. "I promise I won't make up any more stories about Rose."

"All right, Janie," Nancy said. "But if you ever see the woman with the dolls again, please let me know right away." She wrote her name and phone number on a slip of paper.

Nancy was tempted to reveal what she had learned to Mrs. Struthers, then she thought better of it. The woman already was nervous, and knowing that Rose might be in danger would only upset her more.

Instead, Nancy sought her father's advise. He

shared her alarm about Rose's safety and said at once that a detective should be assigned to the Struthers' grounds.

"We can't do that without telling Mrs. Struthers," Nancy replied, "and I don't want to worry her."

"Tell you what," Mr. Drew decided. "I'll engage the detective on my own and tell him not to let the Struthers know he is on duty. After this has blown over, if Mrs. Struthers feels the service has been worthwhile she can pay me for it."

Nancy visited the Struthers' home the next day, where everything appeared to be running smoothly. Rose was bubbling with enthusiasm over her dancing and violin lessons. Her teachers had said she had talent, and Mrs. Struthers was pleased.

"Perhaps a career in music is ahead for my granddaughter," she predicted enthusiastically to Nancy when they were alone. "And I have you to thank, my dear."

"I'm glad I've done something helpful," Nancy said, "even though I haven't found the doll you want. But I did buy two things at the Jefferson Galleries."

She handed Mrs. Struthers the package containing the four-faced doll and the album with the name of Euphemia Struthers on it.

"What an interesting doll!" the woman remarked after turning it round and round. "I haven't seen one like this before. It will be a great addition to my collection. And this album—how quaint! Euphemia? Let me see. My husband had an unmarried cousin by that name."

"Where does she live?" Nancy asked eagerly.

"In some suburb of New York City. I've forgotten exactly where."

Nancy examined the album thoroughly a second time but found nothing that might help her to solve the mystery. She looked up to find Mrs. Struthers with a faraway expression in her eyes.

"Could you go to New York for me?" she asked abruptly.

"New York? Why, yes, I guess so," Nancy replied. "You mean to see Euphemia Struthers?"

"If you can find her. But also to attend a large sale of exquisite old dolls," the woman said.

Nancy's mind immediately flew to various possibilities in connection with the trip. First, her Aunt Eloise Drew, who lived in New York, had been coaxing her to visit. Also, her friend Alice Crosby, a social-service worker in the city, had expressed a desire to see the young detective.

"How I wish I might go myself." Mrs. Struthers sighed. "Alfred Blackwell is giving a recital."

"He is?" Nancy said. "I'd love to hear him." To herself she added, "And I'll try to have an interview with him. Since he's a violinist, he may have known Rose's father and possibly can tell me where Romano is now." Aloud she said, "Yes, I'll go. When is the sale?"

"In a few days."

The next morning Nancy left for New York. When she arrived in the city, she went at once to the suburban telephone directories and looked for the name Struthers.

"Here it is! Euphemia Struthers."

She made a call and the woman herself answered.

"This is Nancy Drew from—"

"It is, eh? Well, it's about time I heard from you!" the woman said.

CHAPTER VII

A Helpful Gift

NANCY was so startled by Euphemia Struthers' unexpected words that she was speechless.

"I thought your conscience would bother you one of these days," the tirade began. "I want that album of mine back and I want it right away!"

Nancy was dumbfounded. How had the woman found out that she had bought the album? The thought struck her that she must have picked up some stolen property!

As Miss Struthers paused for breath, Nancy said, "Please let me speak. I don't know how you found out about the album. I don't have it, but I assure you it's in good hands. Mrs. John Struthers of River Heights is the new owner."

"What did you do with the pictures?" Euphemia screamed. "She hasn't got them, too! Oh, no!"

"There weren't any in the album," Nancy said.

"What do you mean?"

At last Nancy was able to describe the whole transaction. When she finished Miss Struthers asked in a subdued voice, "Who did you say you are?"

Nancy gave her name very clearly. A great gasp came from the telephone along with a profuse apology.

"Oh, my goodness, I thought you said 'Nanny Dew,' that thieving maid of mine! If I ever get my hands on that girl. . . ."

"Your time is up," an operator's voice cut in. "If you wish to talk longer, deposit. . . ."

"I don't!" Nancy said, and hung up. She leaned against the side of the telephone booth and laughed. "Whew! I'm glad that's over! The clue didn't get me anywhere, but I'll see that Miss Euphemia Struthers' album is returned to her. I wonder what Nanny Dew did with the photographs?"

Nancy pushed the door of the booth open and went direct to the taxi stand. Ten minutes later she rang the bell of her aunt's apartment. Miss Drew, an attractive middle-aged schoolteacher, greeted Nancy with open arms.

"This is the nicest thing that's happened to me this vacation," Aunt Eloise said, as she helped her niece unpack the few clothes she had brought along.

"Either you don't intend to stay long or you left home in a hurry," Miss Drew teased.

"Neither. Guess again." Nancy laughed. "I'm going shopping."

"That doesn't sound like you, Nancy. Are you sure there isn't some other reason for this visit?"

"I see I can't keep secrets from you, Aunt Lou!"

Nancy described her new mystery and her hope of tracing Romano Pepito through Alfred Blackwell by questioning him after the concert the next evening.

"I'll get tickets for us," Aunt Eloise offered.

Nancy spent a happy evening with her aunt and the next day they shopped for several hours. Nancy purchased a dress to wear to the concert. She and Miss Drew arrived early, and Nancy handed the usher a note to take to the violinist.

Nancy thought Blackwell's playing was even more wonderful than it had been when she heard him in River Heights. Just before the second half of the program began, the usher gave Nancy an answer to her note. It invited the girl and her aunt to go backstage to see the artist immediately after the concert.

"Now if he can only give me a clue to the Struthers' mystery!" she thought, excited.

When they met Alfred Blackwell he not only remembered having met Nancy in River Heights but expressed great pleasure that she and her aunt had come to hear him. They in turn told the violinist how much they had enjoyed his performance. Then Nancy explained the purpose of her request to see him.

"Romano Pepito?" Mr. Blackwell repeated. "Ah, yes, I know him. I've heard him play many times. He is a fine violinist. His music expresses the depths of gloom and the heights of joy so well known to gypsies."

"Where is he now?" Nancy asked.

"That I could not say. I haven't seen him for over three years. You know him?"

"No, but I'd like to meet Mr. Pepito."

"Perhaps I can help you. Can you and your aunt come to my hotel tomorrow morning?"

Nancy looked at her aunt, who nodded assent. At eleven o'clock the following day they went to the violinist's suite. He greeted them cordially but said he had disappointing news.

"I couldn't find out anything about Romano Pepito," he said. "The man seems to have vanished from the music world, though there has been no report of his death."

Mr. Blackwell picked up a photograph and handed it to Nancy. "A very good picture of Romano," he explained. "Isn't he handsome?"

"He certainly is. It's important that I find him."

"If this picture will help you, please take it," Alfred Blackwell offered. "Is Romano in some kind of trouble?"

"Not that I know of," Nancy answered evasively. "I'm interested in all talented gypsies."

Alfred Blackwell nodded as if satisfied with the explanation. "In that case you must meet my friend Marquita," he said.

"You mean the movie actress?" Nancy's aunt inquired. "She was very good in her latest film."

"Yes, her new picture is to open here this week. Marquita is a Spanish gypsy, and one of the most unselfish, beautiful women I have ever known."

"Is she in New York now?" Nancy asked.

"I believe so. Wait, I'll find out."

The violinist called the theatrical agent who arranged all Marquita's engagements. From him Mr. Blackwell learned that the actress had arrived the day before.

"We'll go to her apartment," Alfred Blackwell decided impulsively. "She refuses to have a phone, or I'd call her."

He and the two Drews taxied to the actress's apartment. To Nancy's amazement Marquita did not reside in an exclusive neighborhood.

"Marquita makes a large salary but spends little of it on herself," the violinist explained. "I sometimes wonder if it isn't because she's compelled to turn over the major part of her earnings to the Gypsy group of which she remains a member."

The woman, dark, beautiful, and exotic looking, opened the door. She wore plain, inexpensive clothes. Her apartment also was sparsely furnished. Marquita greeted them cordially.

Before she had a chance to ask her callers to be seated, Mr. Blackwell said, "Suppose we all go to lunch to that famous Hungarian restaurant on the next block."

Marquita offered no protest, and the Drews' objections were quickly overridden. At the restaurant Alfred Blackwell ordered a full-course meal for each one.

Nancy sought to draw Marquita into a discussion of gypsy customs and superstitions. The actress answered the questions politely but reluctantly. She could give no information about Romano Pepito and seemed disinterested in the subject of dolls or albums.

"Gypsies do not have albums," she said.

Nancy made a final attempt to get a clue from Marquita by asking whether gypsies who had been banished from a tribe could be reinstated.

"The old tribal law is becoming more liberal," Marquita admitted. "It depends on the tribe, though. Some leaders allow certain members to go out into the world. Others are not allowed to leave."

Out of consideration for her host, Nancy did not pursue the subject. The rest of the lunch hour was gay, and the guests were profuse in their thanks to Alfred Blackwell for his kindness.

The next morning Nancy and her aunt went to the doll sale. Several fine ones were on display. Many duplicated those already in Mrs. Struthers' collection, but one caught Nancy's attention. She listened carefully to a description of it when the auctioneer put the doll up for sale.

He explained that it dated back to Civil War days and had been used to carry messages and even quinine medicine through enemy lines. He demonstrated how the head could be removed by a sudden quick turn. Beneath it was a cavity where the precious drug and notes had been secreted.

"There's a story that children were allowed to visit their fathers who were war prisoners of the enemy. They carried the dolls through the lines, and no one suspected that they were helping their parents trick the enemy," he continued. "A guaranteed authentic collector's item! Now what am I offered?"

"I believe I'll buy that for Mrs. Struthers' collection if the bidding doesn't go too high," Nancy whispered to her aunt.

Several persons made bids. As the price rose, everyone dropped out except Nancy and a woman at the rear of the room.

"She sounds like Nitaka!" Nancy thought, turning around.

The woman wore a large hat and scarf that covered the side of her face. "Maybe she wants that doll because it has something to do with the Struthers' case," Nancy reasoned.

Quickly the girl made another bid for the doll. The woman topped her offer by a large amount. Nancy raised the bid, but this time her competitor said nothing.

The auctioneer called, "Sold to the young lady down front!"

The woman at the rear of the room muttered angrily and departed.

"She *is* Nitaka!" Nancy decided, as the gypsy's

scarf blew aside and revealed her carrot-colored hair.

Nancy decided to follow the woman. Quickly she explained her plan to her aunt and asked Miss Drew to pay for the doll and take it home with her.

"Please be careful," Aunt Eloise pleaded.

"I will. Meet you at the apartment."

Nancy trailed the gypsy to a subway station, where she nearly lost Nitaka as the woman boarded a train. The young sleuth dashed in just as the door closed. When Nitaka left the train, fifteen minutes later, Nancy climbed the stairs to the street a short distance behind her.

The woman turned into a large but shabby-looking apartment house. Nancy reached the building a few seconds later, but could find no trace of Nitaka in the dimly lighted hall.

Annoyed and puzzled, she questioned a group of children who were playing on the sidewalk. They had not noticed the woman. On a sudden hunch Nancy asked them if any gypsies lived in the building.

"Are you a policewoman?" one of the boys demanded, his eyes showing fright.

"No, I'm not."

"Did you come to have your fortune told?"

"If I can find a gypsy to read my palm, I will," Nancy answered. She hoped the boy could lead her to Nitaka.

"My grandmother tells fortunes," the lad declared.

"You're not a gypsy, are you?"

"Sure I am, and so's my grandmother. She tells swell fortunes, only the police won't let her charge anything. 'Course if you like the fortune you can give her a gift. The police wouldn't care about that."

"I see," Nancy said. "Where is your grandmother?"

"Upstairs. Come on, I'll show you."

The dark-eyed boy motioned for Nancy to follow him inside. Excited, she started across the sidewalk after him. Then she paused. Would she run into danger if Nitaka should catch sight of her?

"Come on!" the boy urged. "My grandmother won't see anybody after twelve o'clock and it's five minutes to twelve now!"

Nancy felt that there might possibly be some connection between Nitaka and the old gypsy woman. If she did not follow this very minute, she would miss her chance!

CHAPTER VIII

The Fortuneteller's Trick

As NANCY hesitated another moment and debated what to do, someone called her name. She turned and saw a young woman in a blue suit.

"Why, Alice, where in the world did you come from?" she cried.

"Nancy Drew! It's good to see you again. What a wonderful surprise!" Alice Crosby exclaimed. She was the friend whom Nancy had intended to look up. The young woman said she was investigating a social-service case in the neighborhood.

"And what are you doing here?" she asked.

"I was just going to have my fortune told by a gypsy," Nancy replied with a significant wink. "Want to join me?"

"You bet I will. I'd love to have my fortune told, too." She winked back.

The friends followed the boy up the stuffy, dirty stairway to the third floor. From behind a closed door came the voices of two women quarreling. They spoke partly in Romany, partly in English.

"We need money for the Cause, I tell you! No excuses!" one of them said.

Nitaka!

"You are behind in your payments! I must have at least one hundred dollars!" she cried.

"Oh, we are poor. We have no money," the other woman said with a whine. "The police stopped me from working. We can't even get enough money for food!"

"Food! Is not salvation for all of us more important? Give me the money!"

As Nancy listened, her pulses quickened. Why was Nitaka demanding money? What was the Cause?

"Wait here," the gypsy boy said. "I'll tell Grandmother you want your fortune told."

Before Nancy could restrain him, the boy burst through the door, shouting, "Customers!"

Instantly there was a hubbub inside. Chairs were pushed about and a door slammed. It was a few minutes before anyone appeared to greet the callers. Then a bent old woman hobbled into the outer room where Alice and Nancy stood. She had on a red flared skirt, and a yellow silk scarf draped completely over her head, face, and blouse.

"Hello, my pretties," she cackled in a high-pitched voice.

"We've come to have our fortunes told," Nancy said.

"You come too late," the gypsy croaked. "No longer do I take money for telling fortunes. The police will not allow it."

"But you could accept a gift?"

"What do you offer?"

Nancy took an attractive gold chain from her purse. The gypsy's dark eyes gleamed.

"Sit down!" she ordered and pushed Nancy into a chair. "I will tell only one fortune—yours. Give me your gift."

Nancy handed over the chain. The gypsy took the girl's hand in her own and stared fixedly at the lines. Nancy in turn gazed down at the fortuneteller's hands. She was surprised to note that the flesh was as firm and hard as that of a young person.

"You do not live in New York," the gypsy said rapidly in her raspy voice. "I see you come here on a special mission to find someone. Am I right?"

"Possibly."

"You seek to find that which never will come to you," the woman continued. "If you value your life, you will return quickly to your home and stay there. Good times lie ahead of you. I see much money, but only if you give up your present search and cease meddling in the affairs of others!"

"Interesting," Nancy commented. She decided upon a bold move. "As it happens, I came to this very house to find a woman named Nitaka. I wish to talk to her."

The gypsy's hand jerked away from hers.

"Nitaka has gone!" she muttered. Then, as an afterthought, she added, "She has not been here for a long time."

"I don't believe that," Nancy replied, "because I heard her voice a few minutes ago. She must be in this apartment!"

"Nitaka is not here!" the gypsy repeated. "You do not believe me? Then look around and let your eyes tell you so."

Nancy needed no second invitation. She opened a door to an adjoining room and walked in. Alice followed her. Huddled in a dark corner was an old gypsy woman. She was fully dressed except for a skirt.

Instantly Nancy realized that a trick had been played on her. The fortuneteller outside was not the gypsy lad's grandmother, but Nitaka! She had put on the older woman's skirt, and had hidden her face under the scarf!

Too late Nancy wheeled. Already Nitaka had disappeared into the hall. She had stripped off the skirt and scarf, which lay on the floor.

"Stop her, Alice!" Nancy urged.

The two girls rushed to the door but Nitaka was almost at the foot of the lowest stairway. All they could see was the top of her head. A moment later the carrot-haired woman reached the street.

"No use following her," Alice advised. "And I must leave soon."

She and Nancy went back to the apartment to find out what they could about Nitaka from the old gypsy and the little boy. After persistent questioning, they learned that Nitaka had been there several times. She tried to force them to pay tribute.

"Why do you give her money?" Nancy asked.

"We are afraid not to." The old grandmother sighed. "Nitaka says the king of all gypsies will harm us if we do not obey her."

"I don't think you need worry any more," Nancy said kindly. "Surely Nitaka will not come back here to bother you now that we've found her out." She turned to Alice and whispered, "I think we'd better report Nitaka to the authorities."

The girls left the apartment and hurried down the creaking stairs to the street.

"My, it's good to breathe fresh air again!" Alice remarked. "It was terribly smelly up there. I'll bet those rooms haven't been cleaned and aired in a long time. I must look into that situation. Those people probably need help."

"Do you know where the nearest police station is?" Nancy asked.

Alice, familiar with this part of the city, led Nancy to one a few blocks away. A pleasant lieutenant at the desk greeted them. The girls told him about Nitaka and suggested that the police watch for her on the chance she might return.

"I'll send a plainclothesman over there at once," he promised.

Nancy and Alice thanked him and left. The girls chatted for a while. Then, after making a date to meet for lunch the next day, they parted.

As Nancy walked toward the subway station, she found herself intrigued by the stores. In the window of a small antique shop several plush-covered albums were on display. "I'll go inside and ask about them," she decided.

The old storekeeper was not pleasant. "It's a nuisance to get things out of the window!" he complained. "Folks always want to look, and never buy! I'm getting plumb tired of it!"

"I'll buy one if I find the kind I'm looking for," Nancy told him.

Grudgingly the man got them out one by one. He observed Nancy's disappointed expression as she fingered through the albums. He offered her several others, which he took from beneath the counter. One had a red morocco-leather cover, trimmed in bands of gold leaf, with a gilt fastener. Another was of faded-blue satin with an ivory clasp and tiny yellow rosebuds painted on it.

"This old blue one contains verses," the man said. "Silly stuff. But you could tear out the pages and put in new ones," he suggested.

The shopkeeper thumbed through the album to a passage, which he read, " 'For if kith and kin and all had sworn, I'll follow the gypsy laddie.' Now does that make sense?"

"I think it does," Nancy said, excited. "A person who had decided to take up his lot with the gypsies might have written it. May I see the album, please?"

Unable to hide her eagerness, Nancy scanned the pages. On the very last one she was astounded to come across a familiar quotation. Written in bold black ink was the sentence:

> *The source of light will heal all ills,*
> *but a curse will follow him who takes*
> *it from the gypsies.*
> *Henrietta Bostwick*

It was the same quotation that Mrs. Struthers had found in her album!

Thrilled by the discovery, Nancy turned back to the first page. A name, probably that of the original owner, had been written there, but the ink had faded and she could not decipher it.

"This album must have an interesting history," Nancy remarked to the shopkeeper. "Where did you get it?"

"Oh, it came in a barrel of stuff from another antique shop. The place was going into bankruptcy, so I took part of the stock."

Nancy bought the album and left the shop with mingled feelings of elation and defeat. Because of the strange quotation she was convinced that the unknown Henrietta Bostwick must have some connection with the Pepito family. How could she trace her?

Nancy passed the public library and on impulse went in. For two hours she pored over records on genealogy but could find no Bostwick family listing Henrietta as a member. After she had perused all the volumes on this subject, she returned to her aunt's apartment.

"Oh, Nancy, I'm so glad you've come!" Miss Drew exclaimed as her niece entered the foyer. "I've been so worried."

"Worried? Why, Aunt Lou, you know I can find my way around New York without a bit of trouble."

"I haven't been worried about you, Nancy. It's a package that came."

Nancy looked at the package lying on the table. It was addressed to her.

As she reached for it her aunt cried out, "No! No! Don't touch it!"

"Why not, Aunt Lou?"

"A woman telephoned less than half an hour ago," her aunt explained, excited. "She refused to give her name, but she warned me that it would be very dangerous for you to open the package!"

CHAPTER IX

A Strange Dismissal

NANCY looked closely at the package without touching it. Although clearly addressed to her, the sender's name did not appear, and it had not been sent by mail or express.

"How did it come?" she asked her aunt.

"Up the dumbwaiter. Fifteen minutes after the package was delivered the mysterious phone warning came. Nancy, we must call the police!"

"Yes," her niece agreed and reached for the telephone.

Within a few minutes two detectives were at the apartment. They examined the package.

"There might be a bomb in it," one officer announced.

"But there's no ticking sound," Nancy protested. "In spite of the warning, the package may be perfectly harmless. I'd hate to ruin the contents unless it were necessary."

"I agree," the other detective said.

"Okay, we'll open it," his companion agreed, "but not here. We'll take it back to headquarters for a test."

Nancy and her aunt went along. They were fascinated by the detection gadget.

"Guess the package won't pop," the police officer said. "If the contents are dangerous, it's for some other reason."

The man untied the string, and removed the heavy brown wrapping paper.

"Can't see a thing yet," he muttered. "Well, here goes!"

He raised the cover of the box an inch and peered into the crack. Then with an exclamation of disgust, he threw off the top.

"Look what's inside! Nothing but a doll! You've called the police for this!" he chided the Drews.

With a gesture of contempt, the detective started to pick up the doll. Nancy darted forward and cried, "Don't touch that! It's dangerous!"

"Dangerous? What do you mean?" the officer asked.

"It contains a drug! This witch doll was stolen a few days ago in Jefferson."

"You're sure?"

"I never saw the doll until now," Nancy answered, "but I believe it's the one. Perhaps you'd better check with the owner of the Jefferson Galleries to make sure."

"We'll do that," the detective decided as he replaced the box cover.

"Any idea who sent you the package, and why?" his buddy asked.

Nancy was evasive. In her own mind she was satisfied that the doll was the stolen one and had been sent as an offering of ill will by Nitaka. Since she had no proof, the girl detective did not want to give the gypsy's name to the police.

She wondered who could have telephoned the friendly warning. It was evident that her present address was no secret to at least two people who did not wish to make themselves known to her.

After leaving police headquarters, Nancy said to her aunt, "Nitaka probably saw me on the street and followed me to your apartment," she said. "But I can't imagine who my unknown friend is."

"Whoever she is," Miss Drew replied, "I'm thankful to her, and certainly relieved that no harm came to you."

Nancy spent another day in New York and had lunch with Alice Crosby. Then the following morning, despite her aunt's insistence that she stay longer, Nancy felt that she should get back to River Heights and work on the mystery. She caught an afternoon plane and reached home in time for dinner. After telling her father and Hannah Gruen of her adventures, she telephoned George.

"I'm back from the big city," she said. "How's everything?"

"Bess and I have lots to tell you. Suppose we stop by in the morning?"

"I planned to see Mrs. Struthers," Nancy explained. "I brought her an interesting old album with that strange 'source of light' message in it."

"Well, I may have a clue for you," George said. "Want to know the location of a gypsy camp with a violinist?"

"Do I!"

"Then Bess and I will pick you up about ten o'clock and show you where it is."

George and Bess arrived at the Drew home exactly at ten. Nancy hopped into the car and the three were off on a search.

"We knew you'd be interested," Bess said, as they rode along. "Someone was playing a violin when we passed the camp the other day. We didn't see who it was, but the music was beautiful."

Nancy asked a dozen eager questions, but the cousins could tell her little about the group. They had noticed it while driving through a distant town two days before.

"I hope the gypsies are still there!" Nancy said.

In a short while the girls reached their destination and climbed out of the car. Several gypsy children were playing close by. They began chattering, and some ran off, evidently to tell their parents that visitors had arrived.

Nancy walked over to the remaining group. As the children stared at her, she asked if they knew a man named Romano Pepito. Soberly the children shook their heads.

Nancy took a package of gum from her pocket. "This is for the first boy or girl who tells me the name of your violinist!" she announced.

"Murko!" several cried in unison.

Nancy split the package of gum, so that each child received a stick. "Now lead me to Murko," she requested.

"Nobody but gypsies can see him," one little girl said. "It's not allowed."

At this point a pretty woman, with bangles in her ears and bracelets jingling, appeared from a tent and came swiftly to the group. The girls expected to be ordered to leave. Instead, the gypsy smiled and offered to tell their fortunes.

"Have you a license to tell fortunes?" Nancy inquired.

"Yes, I have," the woman answered. She reached out as if to take the girl's hand. "Shall I read your future?"

"No thank you. I've had my fortune told recently," Nancy replied.

Just then the strains of violin music came from one of the trailers at the far end of the camp. Nancy's expression revealed her interest.

"I'd like to meet Murko," she said.

The gypsy woman looked at her intently, shook her head, and whispered, "Gypsy music fills the air. Listen and you will learn. But never try to pierce their secrets, or misfortune will befall you!" She turned and walked swiftly toward the cluster of trailers.

"Now what did she mean by that?" Bess asked nervously.

"I think she was telling us to move on and ask no more questions about the violinist," George remarked.

"Then let's make tracks," Bess urged.

"Not so fast," Nancy pleaded. "I've not learned half enough." She searched in her pocketbook and pulled out some lifesavers. She held them up for the children to see and asked, "How many of you have dolls?"

All the little girls bobbed their heads.

"Show them to me, will you please, and then I'll give you some candy," Nancy coaxed.

With a shout, the children ran off to the trailers. Soon they returned with their treasured possessions. One quick glance and Nancy knew none of them was the special doll Mrs. Struthers wanted. Most of them were made of rough, unpainted wood. One, with a wax face, had a ludicrous expression. The wax had evidently been cracked in places by cold weather and melted in others by the sun.

"You must have lots of fun with these babies of yours," Nancy said kindly.

"They're not very pretty," one little girl spoke up. "You ought to see Nitaka's dolls! They're beautiful."

Nancy was careful to keep her voice steady as she asked, "Where is Nitaka?"

"Gone," the child said with a shrug.

"Nitaka always comes and goes," another child contributed as she sucked on a lifesaver Nancy had offered. "She never stays long."

"Nitaka comes and goes alone?" Nancy probed. "Sometimes, perhaps, with a man?"

"With Anton," the child with the wax doll answered.

"And Zorus? Does he live here?"

"The king of the gypsies?" the little girl said with awe. "He went—"

Before she could say any more, a bell tinkled and all the children scampered off. Nancy wondered if they had been called away purposely.

"Let's go before someone comes after us," Bess urged nervously.

At that moment the violinist began to play again, this time "Gypsy Love Song." The music seemed to come from the farthest tent.

"Never try to pierce the gypsies' secrets, or misfortune will befall you!" the woman whispered.

"Girls, I must meet that man!" Nancy exclaimed. "He may be Romano using another name!"

"No! Don't try it!" Bess warned. "No telling what might happen to you!"

"Remember the gypsy woman's warning," George added fearfully. "Please don't."

But Nancy was gone. Fearlessly she hurried toward the musician's trailer.

CHAPTER X

Complications

BEFORE Nancy could reach the trailer the violin music was coming from, a stout, ugly woman ran toward her.

"Go!" she ordered harshly. "You are not welcome here!"

Dogs began to bark. Men and women poured from the trailers and walked toward Nancy. She found herself completely hemmed in by unfriendly faces.

"Go!" the woman shouted again. "And do not return!"

"I mean no harm," Nancy said, stalling for time. "I only wish to meet the violinist."

"It is forbidden."

Nancy realized from the grim faces about her that argument was useless. Accordingly she left.

"Let's get away from here as fast as possible!" Bess pleaded as George started the car.

"The violinist probably wasn't Romano anyway," George said philosophically. "And say, I'm about starved. What say we stop at Wrightville for a bite?"

Half an hour later they ate in a pleasant tearoom, and then went to look in the windows of several quaint stores. One antique shop with dolls on display drew their attention. As they started to go inside, a man came out of the store. He clasped a small bundle against his coat pocket.

Startled, Nancy said to her friends, "Girls, that's the purse snatcher!" She darted after him. "Come on! We mustn't let him get away this time!"

The fellow realized that Nancy had recognized him and ran to the corner, where a blue sedan had just stopped. He jumped inside, and a second later the vehicle pulled from the curb.

"We must follow him!" Nancy exclaimed.

Bess suggested that she wait in town while Nancy and George track down the thief. The other girls agreed and jumped into George's car.

From the outset, the chase was hopeless. There was a traffic tie-up and when that cleared, George could not find the blue car. She insisted that they turn around and pick up Bess.

When they found her, she giggled. "Who says I'm not a super detective? While you two were gone, I went back to the antique shop where we saw the purse snatcher and got some information about him."

"What was it?" Nancy asked eagerly.

"The man sold a doll to the dealer for one hundred and fifty dollars."

"Did you see the doll?" Nancy asked, excited.

"Yes, it was an Early American rag doll. Its hands were made of kid gloves and it had shoe buttons for eyes. The dealer said that the face had been painted on with vegetable dyes. For the life of me, I can't see why anyone would pay such a fancy price for a rag doll!"

"Because they're so rare," Nancy explained.

"It was kind of cute at that," Bess admitted. "The doll's hair was made of yellow string. Its dress was an India-print skirt with a little home-spun linen jacket."

"I remember seeing one like that in Mrs. Struthers' collection!" Nancy exclaimed. "I wonder if the thief stole it from her."

"He had a package with him when he left the shop," George reminded the others. "What do you suppose was in it? Something else he stole?"

"The shopkeeper," Bess went on, "said the man had another doll with him to sell, but the dealer didn't want to buy it."

Nancy decided to telephone Mrs. Struthers to find out if the doll just purchased by the antique dealer belonged to her. When she described the doll, Mrs. Struthers said it did not.

"I have one exactly like it except for the India-print dress," the woman said. "My doll is safe. The one sold must be—"

Before Mrs. Struthers could continue, Rose cut in on an extension telephone and eagerly told Nancy about her music and dancing lessons.

"Oh, I just love them!" she shouted. "My teacher says I'm a natural. I'm to have an audition for television or the movies if Granny will say it's okay."

"Granny hasn't said so yet," Mrs. Struthers interrupted. "Rose is not doing so well with her other lessons, Nancy, and until she does I couldn't think of such a thing."

"I can't study all the time!" Rose exclaimed. "Anyway, it's just like being in jail here. I can't leave the house without being watched."

"Why, what do you mean?" Mrs. Struthers asked.

"I know you put a detective on the grounds. He watches me all the time. I don't like it. Everybody in this house is being watched."

Dismayed that Rose had learned about the detective Mr. Drew had employed, Nancy tried to calm the girl and her grandmother. Of course Mrs. Struthers professed her innocence.

"Please don't worry," Nancy pleaded. "I'm responsible for this, and I'll explain everything when I see you."

Alarmed at the turn affairs had taken, Nancy and her friends returned home. Several hours elapsed before the young detective reached the Struthers' house.

When Nancy arrived, she learned that her telephone call had caused a lot of confusion in the household. Rose's conversation had been overheard by Mrs. Carroll, who had promptly repeated it to her husband.

Convinced that a detective had been employed because the couple was thought to be dishonest, the woman had announced that they were leaving at once. To pacify them, Mrs. Struthers had ordered the detective off the grounds.

Nancy's explanation of why her father had engaged the man without first speaking to Mrs. Struthers cleared matters somewhat. Rose's grandmother said she appreciated the Drews' good intentions, but did not want the detective to return.

Nancy changed the subject. "I've brought some purchases, and also a photograph of Romano Pepito," she said.

Mrs. Struthers' eyes opened wide. "I've never seen a picture of him. Is he—"

Nancy smiled as she handed over the picture. "He's very handsome and kind looking. I'm sure he wouldn't harm anyone intentionally. No doubt he was forced to leave his family against his will."

Mrs. Struthers gazed at the photograph for several seconds before speaking. Tears filled her eyes. "I—I do so wish things had been different," she said. "Yes, he is handsome. Rose looks like him and no doubt inherits his musical talent. But the fire in her—"

"What fire?" asked a voice, and Rose danced into the room. Seeing the photograph, she cried out, "Who's this? Don't tell me! I know! It's my father!"

"What makes you think so?" Nancy countered, giving Mrs. Struthers a chance to decide whether or not to tell her granddaughter the truth.

"Because I look like him!" Rose said.

Nancy glanced at Mrs. Struthers, who put her arm around the child and said, "Yes, he is your father."

"I want to see him!" Rose demanded. "Take me to him."

"We do not know where he is—or do you, Nancy?" the woman asked hopefully.

Nancy shook her head.

"Oh, please find him," Rose begged.

"I'll try to," the young detective promised.

As Rose claimed the picture for herself and went off with it, Nancy explained to Mrs. Struthers how she had obtained the photograph and what she was doing to locate Romano Pepito.

"Have you ever heard of a Henrietta Bostwick?" she asked.

"No," Mrs. Struthers answered as Nancy opened the package with the old album in it, and showed her the strange message, which was a duplicate of the one in her own album.

The source of light will heal all ills, but a curse will follow him who takes it from the gypsies.

"What a coincidence!" Mrs. Struthers exclaimed. "I never heard of the woman."

"This Henrietta Bostwick may have sent the same quotation to your daughter."

"That's so," Mrs. Struthers agreed.

She and Nancy discussed the mystery from various angles, but arrived at no conclusion. Nancy then told her how she had chased a man in Wrightville whom she thought was the purse snatcher.

"Sorry I didn't catch him," she said.

"Oh, Nancy, I meant to tell you," Mrs. Struthers interrupted. "The police telephoned this morning. They know the thief's name."

"They do?"

"They believe he's Tony Wassell, a half-breed gypsy. The police followed the tip given by the guard at the museum and traced the purse snatcher through bank records."

"So Tony Wassell is a half-breed gypsy," Nancy remarked thoughtfully. "I'll bet he steals and sells valuable old dolls, as well as other things, and hides in a nearby gypsy camp. I'll tell the state police!" She phoned at once and told the officer where she had seen Wassell and where she thought he might be found.

"If only the man could be captured before he has a chance to use the information contained in the purse!" Mrs. Struthers said to Nancy when she finished the call.

"You mean he might blackmail or rob you?" the girl detective asked.

"Yes. Oh, I never wanted anyone but Rose to see the letter, and not until after my death. That was why I always carried it with me."

Mrs. Struthers did not explain further and Nancy politely did not question her.

"Some nights I can't sleep, worrying about what may happen," Mrs. Struthers went on. "Some gypsies are so vindictive. I've been told that if their tribal laws are violated by one of their number, they often take revenge on a member of the family. I'm afraid they may try to harm Rose because her father married outside his tribe."

"Please try not to worry about it," Nancy said. She did not add that this very idea had been plaguing her for some time.

The next morning, when Nancy came down to breakfast, there were two letters at her place on the dining-room table.

One of them was postmarked Wrightville, and her name and address had been printed. Puzzled, Nancy tore the envelope open and read the message: "Stay at home, Nancy Drew, and attend to your own business! If you don't, it will be the worse for you!"

CHAPTER XI

A Warning

HANNAH Gruen came into the dining room and knew from Nancy's expression that something was wrong.

"What is it?" she asked. "Not bad news, I hope."

Nancy showed her the warning note. "I can't imagine who could have sent it," she said, "unless it was the purse snatcher."

"Oh, Nancy, I'm so worried!" the housekeeper exclaimed after she had read the anonymous message. "It must have something to do with the case you're working on. Please give up trying to help Mrs. Struthers!"

"I can't let a little note like this frighten me," Nancy said. "Anyway, I think the person who sent it merely means he wants me to stay away from Wrightville."

"Then promise me you will," Hannah begged.

"All right." Nancy laughed and gave the woman an affectionate hug. "Any calls for me while I was in the shower?"

"One from the yacht club, asking for any used clothes we might want to donate."

"Good," Nancy said. "I have a pile of Dad's and my things. I'll run over with them."

"Be careful," Mrs. Gruen urged, as Nancy went out the door.

"I'll be all right," Nancy called as she stepped into her car.

She drove over the heavy bridge that spanned the Muskoka River and headed for the yacht club. The river road was practically deserted.

Suddenly Nancy noticed another automobile a short distance behind her. Though she deliberately slowed down to let it pass, the driver did not attempt to do so. She accelerated. The man behind also put on speed.

"He's following me!" Nancy decided finally. "Maybe there's more to that warning note than I thought!"

She kept the image of the other car in her mirror, and as she approached a sharp and dangerous turn where the road shot up a hill, Nancy was alarmed to see that the driver behind her was getting closer.

Although she pressed the gas pedal to the floor, Nancy could not draw away from the pursuing car. A quarter of a mile from the yacht club it pulled abreast of her, but the man did not try to head Nancy off. Instead, he crowded her inch by inch toward the embankment.

Nancy's heart stood still!

Just then she spotted an opening in the low bushes along the right side of the road fifty feet ahead. She recalled that from there a narrow path ran off at an angle down to the river. It was steep and too narrow for a car, but she must risk taking the path if she could reach it.

"I must hold on until I do!" Nancy thought desperately. "Then I can jump out and run!"

Forty more feet to go! Then thirty!

The two cars were neck and neck. Nancy did not dare take her eyes off the road to see who the man alongside her might be.

Twenty feet! Ten!

Suddenly Nancy swung the wheel over. Her car swerved off the highway, bumped over the uneven side road and, still upright, jerked to a stop. Nancy grabbed the key, jumped out, and ran like a deer toward the yacht club.

A few seconds later she halted. The other driver, taken completely by surprise, had appeared to be on the verge of bringing his own car to a stop and pursuing her. Then, apparently, he decided against this plan, for he picked up speed and soon disappeared from sight.

The car was a black sedan!

Quivering, Nancy sat down on the path to recover from the shock and think things over. Finally she gave up trying to figure out who the man was. She returned to her car and tried to back it onto the road, but the wheels merely spun around in the loose dirt.

"I'll have to get someone to push me," she decided.

She removed the pile of clothes from the car and walked down the path to the yacht club. John Holden, an elderly man who did odd jobs on the grounds, called out a good morning to Nancy.

"Hello, John," she greeted him. "My car's stuck up on the hill. Any chance of getting someone to push it out?"

"Sure thing, Miss Nancy!" he replied with a grin. "How did you get yourself into such a fix?"

"A man in a black sedan forced me off the road," she explained.

"That's no laughing matter. You'd better take care. I'll get a couple of fellows to help me."

Nancy dropped off the used clothes at the yacht club and then returned to her car. It was only after considerable effort that the men managed to get the vehicle up the hill. They warned Nancy to drive slowly in case any damage had been done to the auto. Everything seemed to work perfectly.

When Nancy reached home, Hannah informed her that a woman who did not give her name had called to tell Nancy something very important. She would call back shortly.

Nancy wondered if it had anything to do with the mystery. Was the caller a friend—perhaps the woman who had kept her from being harmed by the witch doll? Or was she another enemy!

As the hours slipped by and the phone did not ring, Nancy told Hannah she thought the message might have been a ruse to keep her at home.

"Well, I'm just as glad," the housekeeper said. "Please heed the warning. Don't invite trouble by going out again today. Why don't you work on the mystery here?"

"A good idea," Nancy agreed, still thinking of her narrow escape in the car. "I'll try solving it in this big overstuffed chair."

She curled up in her father's favorite chair and thoughtfully gazed into space. She went over the puzzle piece by piece. Finally her mind reverted to the groups of gypsies she had encountered and the strange behavior of their leaders.

"There must be some meaning behind it all. Take that woman in the last camp, for instance. She wasn't unfriendly, yet she uttered that strange phrase, 'Gypsy music fills the air. Listen and you will learn.'

"What was she trying to tell me? Was she answering my question about Romano Pepito, perhaps?" Suddenly, as if the young detective's subconscious mind had solved the riddle, an answer came to her.

" 'Gypsy music fills the air!' " she exclaimed. "Why, maybe that woman meant the radio or television! Perhaps Romano Pepito plays over the air!"

Nancy eagerly studied the radio and television programs listed in the newspaper, but she could find no station offering gypsy music. She refused to be discouraged and telephoned several nearby stations to ask if a gypsy violinist ever played on their programs. The answer each time was no.

Nancy was unwilling to give up her search. She obtained a list of stations within a two-hundred-mile radius of River Heights and sat down to write a note of inquiry to each one.

As she wrote, the young detective kept the radio on, absently listening to a musical program. It soon ended and another began. Presently a violinist started to play the *Hungarian Rhapsody*.

Nancy listened. The abandon of his style fascinated her. Suddenly she realized that only recently she had heard the same interpretation of that selection. But where? Then she remembered.

"At the gypsy camp!" she recalled. "Maybe this is the same violinist and I'll hear his name!"

But no name was announced at the end of the program. Nancy raced to the telephone to call the broadcasting studio. Eagerly she inquired the name of the violinist.

"Alfred Dunn," was the polite reply.

"He's a gypsy, isn't he?" Nancy asked.

"Indeed not. Thank you for calling. Please keep listening to our programs."

Another disappointment. Nancy sighed as she put down the phone. "Maybe I'll hear something through one of these letters."

She was about to start for the corner mailbox, when the telephone rang again. This time Ned Nickerson was calling.

"How about a date tomorrow night, Nancy?" he asked. "Say around eight o'clock? The crowd wants to go to the Crow's Nest."

"Sounds great, Ned. You always cheer me up, and I need some cheering up right now. Another clue in this mystery I'm working on has failed."

"I'm sorry," he said. "Keep your chin up till I see you."

The next morning at breakfast an advertisement in the newspaper caught Nancy's eye. "Please don't ask me to stay home again today, Hannah. Here's something I must follow up."

"What is it?"

"There's an ad about a chain of toy agencies in towns around here," Nancy replied. "They lend toys, also repair them. Maybe they have old dolls, and—"

"And you can find a solution to the Struthers mystery!" Hannah supplied good-naturedly. "All right, go ahead, but stay on the main roads."

Nancy spent the rest of the day driving from one shop to another. In each place she looked for a doll that lighted up or wore a jeweled robe. The managers had neither seen nor heard of any that fitted this description.

Finally Nancy came to a small shop in Malvern. As she entered, a repairman, Mr. Hobnail, glanced up from a toy train he was fixing. On the workbench were many dolls and other toys.

"Yes?" he inquired in a weary voice. "If it's repairing you want done, I can't touch it for two weeks. I'm head over heels in work now."

Nancy told him of her interest in old dolls. As she spoke, her eyes moved from one object to another in the cluttered little room and came to rest on the toy figure of a man holding part of a violin.

"That doll!" she exclaimed suddenly. "Tell me, please, where did you get it?"

Old Mr. Hobnail scarcely looked up from his work. "Woman named Mrs. Barlow," he answered. "Fixing that violin's to be my next job."

"Have you her address?"

"Certainly," the old man snapped. "I always keep addresses of my customers. She lives at the corner of Beach and Chestnut."

Nancy felt that the doll might be the one Nitaka had carried in the suitcase that had fallen open when she was questioning Janie and the other children.

The young detective thanked the toy repairman and drove to Mrs. Barlow's home. She proved to be a pleasant person, and told Nancy how she had obtained the doll.

"I bought it from a woman who came to my house," Mrs. Barlow said. "Not until she had gone did I notice that the little violin was about to come apart, so I took it to Mr. Hobnail."

"Do you know the woman's name?"

"She didn't give it to me."

"Please describe her?"

"She was a very vivid individual—well groomed. She wore a tailored suit. Her skin was dark, but her hair was, well, I guess you'd call it carrot-colored."

"She must have been a gypsy named Nitaka!" Nancy exclaimed. "I know she had such a doll."

"Who is Nitaka?"

Nancy told a little of what she knew about the gypsy and hinted that she might be a thief.

"Oh, dear!" Mrs. Barlow became worried. "I hope I haven't bought a stolen doll!"

"Not necessarily," Nancy reassured her. "I do wish I could locate that woman, though."

Mrs. Barlow suddenly brightened. "I just thought of something. The woman said she might come back again tonight with another doll!"

"What time?" Nancy asked.

"About seven-thirty. Why don't you stay?" Mrs.

Barlow invited. "We can have dinner together."

Nancy did not like to impose upon the woman's good nature, but felt she probably had hit on something important. She accepted the invitation, then phoned Hannah to let her know where she was.

"And when Ned arrives, Hannah, please ask him to come here for me."

Nancy did not want Nitaka to see her car so she parked it in the Barlow garage. At ten minutes to eight the doorbell rang. Mrs. Barlow answered it, confidently expecting the gypsy. The caller was Ned.

Nancy introduced her friend to Mrs. Barlow and told him about the expected visitor. He willingly agreed to delay their leaving. The evening wore on. By nine-thirty it was clear that Nitaka was not coming.

"Something must have made her afraid to come back," Nancy said.

To wait longer seemed useless, so the couple said good night and started out. Since each of them had a car, Ned suggested Nancy go ahead of him, so he could keep watch for anyone who might try to harm her.

Nothing happened, however, and presently the two arrived at the Crow's Nest, the special rendezvous of River Heights' young people. Nancy and Ned joined their friends and ordered cokes.

News had spread that Nancy was absorbed in another mystery. Though she did not deny this, she avoided revealing any details of the case she was working on. Ned was not so secretive.

"If you ask me, Nancy's reverting to her childhood!" he teased. "Dolls are now one of her big interests!"

"But I don't play with them." Nancy laughed.

"That's the mystery," Ned countered.

During the conversation Dot Larken remarked that the River Heights Yacht Club was having a big-little sister picnic at Star Island the next day.

"You're coming, aren't you, Nancy?" she asked.

Nancy had forgotten about the picnic. After a little urging, she said, "Yes, I'll come and bring a girl named Rose Struthers."

Unnoticed in the adjoining booth sat a swarthy couple. At the mention of Rose's name, they exchanged significant glances but said nothing. They remained in the booth until after Nancy and her friends had left the Crow's Nest.

"This is my first day out of jail," Rose announced the next day as she and Nancy rode to the yacht club.

"You'd better not say things like that at the picnic or people will believe you," Nancy cautioned.

At first Rose behaved surprisingly well, and Nancy felt that the training she had suggested was having a good effect. Rose entertained the group with a series of remarkably well-executed dances that showed real talent.

"My teacher's arranging for radio and television auditions for me," she said, boasting.

"Come, Rose," Nancy broke in, and took the girl off for a swim.

Though not a good swimmer, Rose was utterly fearless in the water. She ignored Nancy's request not to go into deep water and struck out for a float. Nancy brought her back to the beach.

When Nancy walked off to speak to a friend, Rose again struck out for deep water. Suddenly she disappeared. Three small girls on shore who had been watching screamed in terror. Nancy plunged into the water to search for her. A second later Rose bobbed up, laughing gleefully.

"Scared you, didn't I?" she shouted. "I was just holding my breath."

When the picnic was over the two girls headed for the Struthers'. At the front door, Rose rang the bell, but no one came to let them in.

"Where is everybody?" Nancy asked.

"That's funny," Rose said. "But I know where to find a key. Come with me!"

She darted to a side porch and found the key behind a shutter. Rose unlocked the door to the room where the doll collection was kept. She pushed it open, then stopped short.

"Why, look at the furniture!" Rose exclaimed. "It's all topsy-turvy!"

Nancy peered through the doorway. Chairs had been pushed out of place. Dresser drawers had been emptied on the floor. The doll cabinet stood open, and there were many vacant spaces on the shelves.

"The house has been robbed!" Nancy cried.

"And I'll bet something awful has happened to my grandmother!" Rose screamed.

CHAPTER XII

An Interrupted Program

FOR A moment Nancy thought Rose had seen Mrs. Struthers, but this was not so.

"Granny said she was going to stay home all day!" the girl cried out. "Maybe those awful people came and took her away!"

Nancy did not comment. She and Rose ran through the lower part of the house, searching for Mrs. Struthers and the servants.

"Listen!" Nancy commanded suddenly.

From upstairs came a muffled cry that sounded like a call for help. The girls rushed to Mrs. Struthers' bedroom.

The door was locked. As Nancy twisted the knob in vain, she again heard the cry.

"Is that you, Mrs. Struthers?" she called loudly.

"Yes! Yes! Let me out!" came a faint cry.

"Oh, what happened to Granny?" Rose wailed.

"There's no key in the door!" Nancy shouted.

She could not understand the reply, but Rose darted across the hall and took a key from the door of another room.

"This'll open it," she said.

Quickly Nancy unlocked Mrs. Struthers' door. The woman was locked in a closet, but the same key fitted that door, too, and she was soon released. Clad in a blue robe, her hair untidy, she stumbled out. Nancy helped her to the bed.

"Have they gone?" Mrs. Struthers asked wildly.

"The burglars? Yes. Perhaps you'd better not talk now," Nancy suggested, seeing how white and nervous the woman was.

"I'm—I'm all right, but what a fright!" Mrs. Struthers said. "Did they—take much?"

Rose spoke up. "A lot of the dolls. Oh, Granny, why did the thieves lock you up?"

"So I couldn't call the police, I guess."

"Where is Mrs. Carroll?" Nancy asked.

"Everyone has gone away. I see it all now. It was a trick. First, someone called to say Mrs. Carroll was wanted at the home of a sick relative. Her husband drove her there. And the burglars must have been aware that Rose was not here."

"Did you see the robbers, Mrs. Struthers?" Nancy asked.

"Only one, but from their voices I know there were two men."

"Please tell me exactly what happened."

"I was in my room taking a nap when I heard

footsteps in the hall. At first I thought Mrs. Carroll had come back. Then I got up to make certain. Before I knew what was happening, a man wearing a mask entered and locked me in the closet. It was dreadful!"

"How long were you in the closet, Granny?" Rose asked, still frightened.

"Easily a half hour. I'd have smothered if it hadn't been for the opening over the door."

"Then the burglars haven't been gone long," Nancy surmised. "Let's see what's been stolen," she suggested.

Mrs. Struthers took a hasty inventory as they went from room to room. Silverware and jewelry had been taken. What upset her most, however, was the discovery that all the gems had been removed from the cover of the treasured family album.

When Mrs. Struthers saw the doll cabinet, she cried out in distress. After a quick count, the collector estimated that at least twenty of her most valuable dolls were gone.

"My mommy's doll is missing!" Rose cried angrily. "The one she played with when she was a little girl."

"Yes. They took that, too," her grandmother said, gazing sadly at the shelf where the doll had stood. "Now why would they steal that one? It had no resale value."

Mrs. Struther's last remark set Nancy thinking. She suspected that the burglars were Anton and another gypsy—perhaps the purse snatcher Tony Wassell. Though they obviously had taken jewels, silverware, and rare dolls to sell, it seemed odd that they had also selected the doll belonging to Rose's mother.

A key turned in the front door. For a moment the three were fearful of more trouble, but the newcomers proved to be the housekeeper and her husband. They were amazed to hear about the robbery, but declared it explained the reason for the fake telephone call.

At Nancy's insistence, Mrs. Struthers got in touch with the police and reported her loss. A few minutes later two detectives arrived.

Nancy felt she could do nothing more for Mrs. Struthers and returned to her own home. As she entered the front hall, she noticed the afternoon mail on the table. One letter was addressed to her. It was from Radio Station KIO, Winchester. She ripped it open eagerly.

"This must be an answer about the gypsy violinist," Nancy thought.

The program director of the small Winchester station had written that a violinist would broadcast the following evening at eight o'clock.

"The man may be a gypsy," he wrote. "In fact, we suspect that he is, though he uses the name

Albert Martin. If you are interested in obtaining additional information, we suggest that you writ to him at our station."

"I'll go there!" Nancy decided. "Dad will take me. This is what I call a lucky break."

Unfortunately Mr. Drew had to go out of town and could not attend the broadcast, but Ned told her he had the day off from camp and he would go.

Scarcely half an hour later Mrs. Barlow telephoned to say she had been down to Mr. Hobnail's shop. She had seen a doll that might have some significance for Nancy.

"It's really a mannequin, but it's only twenty-six inches high," Mrs. Barlow said. "Mr. Hobnail told me it's one of a collection that's carried from place to place. I thought possibly it might belong to some gypsy."

Nancy thanked the woman and said she would look at the mannequin. Then she asked if the red-haired gypsy had called at the house again.

"No," Mrs. Barlow said. "I haven't heard from her."

She also told Nancy that Mr. Hobnail was to be in his shop late that evening, so Nancy asked Ned to stop there with her on the way to Winchester. When they reached the toy shop and Nancy told Mr. Hobnail what she had come to see, he led the way to the rear of the shop.

"There's the mannequin."

He pointed to a doll about two feet high,

dressed as a bridesmaid. She wore a pale blue gown with a bouffant tulle skirt, and a large picture hat. Though intrigued by the doll, Nancy felt sure she was too typically American to belong to gypsies.

"She looks almost real," Nancy said. "Where did you get her, Mr. Hobnail?"

"A young man brought her in to have one of the arms repaired. He said there's a whole set of these dolls dressed like a wedding party—the bride, the groom and the whole works!

"He's a salesman for some dress manufacturer, I believe," Mr. Hobnail went on. "Goes around exhibiting his lady dolls. They're to be shown at Taylor's Department Store in River Heights in a couple of days if you want to see them."

"I must go," Nancy said.

Secretly she was disappointed that the mannequin had no connection with her own quest. Ned reminded her that time was slipping away, so they left at once.

"We'll have to step on it to get to Winchester by eight," Ned said, looking at the car clock.

"It'll be my own fault if we don't get to the broadcast in time," Nancy remarked, "but I hope we can make it."

Ned drove as fast as the law allowed. It was just eight o'clock when the young people reached the KIO building.

Nancy was afraid they would not be permitted

to watch the broadcast, as the program was already on the air. But a young woman at a desk directed them to a small room with a large window through which they could look down into the studio where Mr. Martin, the violinist, was playing. To Nancy's surprise, she and Ned were his only audience.

"That violinist does look like a gypsy," Nancy thought, as they seated themselves. "But he's not Romano."

She decided to speak to him later, nevertheless, and ask him if he knew Rose's father. As she listened attentively to an exquisite number from "The Gypsy Airs," the girl thought to herself, "I hope Hannah is listening at home. It would be a shame for her to miss this beautiful music."

Back in River Heights, Mrs. Gruen was indeed listening. For ten minutes she had sat near the radio, growing more entranced each moment.

"That man is too great an artist not to be playing over a nationwide hookup," she said, half aloud. "I'm amazed he—Oh!"

The violinist had struck a sharp discord. On a high, squeaking note, the playing suddenly ceased. Angrily a voice cried out, "Murko will play no more! I will not have spies watching me! You play tricks!"

Abruptly the program was cut off the air!

CHAPTER XIII

A Strange Present

AT THE broadcasting studio, Nancy and Ned were even more startled than Hannah Gruen. In the midst of a beautiful passage, the gaze of the musician suddenly focused upon them. His eyes blazed. He struck a discord and stopped playing.

The musician pointed his bow at Nancy and cried out, "Murko will play no more! I will not have spies watching me! You play tricks. . . ."

Murko the gypsy violinist! In his excitement "Mr. Martin" had blurted out his real name!

At this moment the program was cut off in the control room. Murko stumbled from the studio. Nancy, too, rushed outside and down a stairway, followed by Ned. On the floor below, the musician was gesticulating wildly with his bow at the studio director, who had come to find out what had happened.

"You break promise to me!" Murko shouted a

the man. "When I sign to play here, you promise no one ever see me! Only hear me! And now, two people in studio. Spies! They follow me now!"

The violinist pointed accusingly at Nancy and Ned in the hallway.

"Take it easy, Mr. Martin," the director said. "I did not know anyone was watching you. But these people meant no harm, I'm sure."

"They come to make trouble!" the musician exclaimed.

"We're not here to harm you," Nancy said. "We just wanted to see you play. One misses so much not watching a great artist like you!"

At these words of praise, Murko calmed down somewhat. Nevertheless, he moved along the hallway, a furtive look in his black eyes.

"Let us drive you to your home, Mr. Martin," Nancy suggested, purposely using his radio name.

"No!" shrieked the man, apparently frightened anew.

"I believe we can help you," Nancy said kindly.

"What can you do for me?" he demanded suspiciously. "There is no help for poor Murko. None."

"Why do you say that?" Nancy asked. As he did not answer, she said, "Is it because you work so hard and are forced to give all your money to Anton and Nitaka?" Murko remained silent. "You are discouraged because all your earnings must go to the Cause?"

Murko's head dropped. "Yes," he muttered bitterly. "Yes, it is so."

"Why don't you refuse to contribute? Surely you realize there's nothing in it for you—any more than for Marquita or Romano Pepito?"

Murko raised his head and looked straight into Nancy's eyes. "No, there is not. Poor Romano," he murmured. "A man broken in spirit."

Nancy's heart started to pound. Was she on the verge of learning about Rose's father?

"Where is Romano now?" she asked.

"Wherever his tribe is—unless they have moved him as they did me."

"What do you mean?" Nancy asked, puzzled.

Murko did not reply. A look of panic suddenly came over his face. As if frightened at having told the visitors too much, he bolted for an elevator, which had stopped at that floor. He dashed in and the door slammed shut.

By the time Nancy and Ned had descended to the main floor in another elevator, Murko was nowhere to be seen. No one could tell them which direction he had taken.

"Guess he gave us the slip," Ned said, disgusted. "If I'd only been quicker."

"It wasn't your fault, Ned," Nancy consoled him, and added, "At least I've found out why the gypsies at that camp wouldn't let anyone see Murko. To the outside world, he is 'Mr Martin.' "

The young people thought perhaps he had fled to his tribesmen so they inquired at the local police station if there were any gypsies in the vicinity. They were told of a camp approximately ten miles distant, off the Woodville Road. Nancy wondered if the group from the carnival was there

"Murko probably is with them, and maybe Anton and Nitaka," she speculated. "Let's try to find the place."

"We're off!" Ned said.

He and Nancy soon discovered that police directions on how to reach the camp had been somewhat sketchy. To find the Woodville Road was easy enough, but to locate the gypsies' encampment was another matter.

"They may have pulled their trailers along any one of these side roads," Nancy commented. "It's so dark and wooded, we probably couldn't see the spot unless we were right on it."

"Looks like a bad storm coming, too," Ned said, as he rolled the window up partway. "That'll make it harder to find."

Suddenly a flash of lightning cut across the inky sky and revealed a mass of ugly, boiling clouds.

"Maybe we'd better postpone our search and start for home," Nancy suggested.

Ned agreed, and turned the car in the narrow road. Before they had traveled two miles, the storm broke. During the slow ride back to River

Heights, the rain came down in torrents. It was not until they reached the Drew home that it stopped.

"Lucky we started back when we did," Nancy commented as she said good night to Ned. "I hope your boys' camp wasn't washed out!"

"If it was, I'll be ready to see you again in the morning," he said, grinning.

Early the next day George and Bess stopped by to see Nancy. She invited them to help her search for the missing gypsies.

George was eager for the adventure, but cautious Bess reminded them of their unpleasant experience some days before.

"You two must like being thrown out by gypsies!" she remarked.

Bess decided to go along, nevertheless, and up to the time they reached Winchester, she was very gay, chatting about a new restaurant she had found in River Heights, to the detriment of her figure. But as they turned up a side road out of town, and learned from a farmer exactly where the gypsies were, she became uneasy.

When the three girls finally reached the wooded spot, though, she sighed in relief. There was no one in sight. The group had departed.

"Maybe Murko will show up at the broadcasting studio sometime today," George suggested as she noted Nancy's disappointment.

"I doubt it, but we'll stop there," Nancy replied. She turned the car back toward Winchester.

A few minutes later they reached the radio station, and were told by the manager that Mr. Martin would broadcast no more. A woman had come there early that morning and left a note from the violinist. The message had merely said he would never again play over that station.

"We had a contract with him, too," the manager said, "but there's nothing we can do about it."

Nancy and the other girls were ready to leave, when he called, "Are you Miss Nancy Drew?" To her yes, he added, "There's something here for you. It was brought by that woman who left the note. She merely said to give it to you."

From an inner office the man brought out a package. Puzzled, Nancy decided to open it at once. Inside was a red, black, and white hand-woven blanket.

"This is strange," she remarked. "Did the woman leave her name?"

"No, I scarcely noticed her, except that she had blue eyes, unlike most gypsies, and was about fifty years old."

Nancy caught up a corner of the blanket. The name H. Bostwick was woven in the blanket in small letters.

"Could she be Henrietta Bostwick?" Nancy wondered, remembering the name on the album she had bought in New York. "If so, is she a gypsy? Or does she merely live with the tribe? And why did she send me this blanket?"

On the way home Nancy discussed the incident with Bess and George. "I feel sure that woman was trying to send me some information."

At home, Nancy seated herself on the living-room floor and examined every inch of the gypsy blanket.

"These figures woven in here and there mean something. I'm sure of it!" she told herself. "If only I could get at the meaning of the thing, I might have a valuable clue!"

An outside door slammed. Hannah came into the room, her arms loaded with packages.

"Shopping is an awful trial—" she began, then exclaimed, "Nancy, where did you get that?"

"It's a gift from a gypsy."

"Destroy it! Get it out of the house!" Hannah cried.

"Why, what's wrong?" the girl asked, amazed. "Look at the letters on it!"

"Letters?"

"They spell 'Beware'!" Hannah pointed to a series of red figures.

From where Nancy was seated the word became a part of the pattern and could not be made out. She jumped up and darted to the housekeeper's side.

"Why, it does!" she agreed. "Hannah, you darling! You're helping me solve this mystery!"

Greatly excited, Nancy twisted and turned the blanket. She tried to find other words hidden in the maze of geometric figures.

"Hannah, do you see anything else?" she asked.

Mrs. Gruen shook her head. She and Nancy walked into the hall to study the blanket from a distance.

Suddenly Nancy exclaimed, "I have it! I see it!" She gave the housekeeper a hug.

"What is it?" Mrs. Gruen asked.

Nancy took a quick step forward and pointed out three more words, "king and sun."

"It says, 'Beware king and sun'!"

"Yes, it does," the woman agreed, "but I don't see any sense in those words."

"There must be a meaning to it all! The word 'king' could refer to Zorus, the gypsy chief! I can't figure out 'sun.' The message might mean, 'Beware of the king and his Son'!"

"You always did have a lively imagination," Mrs. Gruen said.

Nancy scarcely heard her. Thinking aloud, she continued, "if the word is 'son,' who could he be? Anton, perhaps, or maybe Romano, Rose's father?"

"The word isn't 'son,'" Hannah insisted. "It says 'sun,' plain as day. Are gypsies sun worshippers?"

"*Get that blanket out of this house!*" Hannah cried.

Nancy's eyes opened wide. She exclaimed, "Why didn't I think of it before! 'Sun' *is* the word and it means 'source of light'! Beware the King and his source of light!

"Hannah, at long last the light is beginning to dawn."

CHAPTER XIV

The Mannequin's Hint

NANCY rushed to the telephone and called state police headquarters. After identifying herself as Carson Drew's daughter, she said, "Will you please try to locate the gypsies that moved out of Winchester recently? And when you do, will someone from your office go there with me?"

The officer listened carefully as she gave a summary of all the things that had happened in which she thought certain gypsies had been involved. She felt the guilty persons might be hiding in that tribe.

"We'll start searching at once and let you know what we find out," the officer promised.

While waiting to hear from him, Nancy dashed over to Mrs. Struthers' home to show her the strange blanket. Rose was having a music lesson and Nancy could hear the clear, true notes of a violin.

Nancy thought the teacher must be playing, but Mrs. Struthers smiled proudly and said, "That's Rose. Isn't she doing well? And her dancing is remarkable. Oh, Nancy, she's so happy now, and I have you to thank for everything. If only we could find her father and the mysterious doll."

"I have a new idea," Nancy announced. "It came to me after looking at this gift from some strange gypsy woman."

Mrs. Struthers gazed in awe at the blanket and felt sure it carried an unfriendly warning. Nancy said she did not share the woman's anxiety.

"I have a new theory I want to work on. To start I'd like a little more information about your daughter's last illness. Would you mind if I ask the doctor about it?"

"No, indeed. The physician was Dr. Tiffen. I'm sure he'll talk with you, although he always says Enid's illness was a puzzle to him."

Nancy went to Dr. Tiffen's office and learned that the illness was not so much a puzzle as he had pretended to Mrs. Struthers and her daughter.

"I did not think it wise to tell them. I knew Enid could not live long," the doctor revealed. "What did puzzle me, though, was that at times she seemed to have abundant energy, and at others she had almost none."

"You gave her medication?" Nancy asked.

"Oh, yes, but that was to ease the pain. In cases

like hers, I know of nothing to prescribe to give a patient energy."

"Dr. Tiffen," Nancy said, "I have a theory, which may sound crazy, but if you have time, may I tell you what it is?"

"Every once in a while," he said, smiling, "a layman hits upon an idea that is a great boon to mankind." Nancy explained that she had figured out that "source of light" meant the sun. Since energy comes from the sun, possibly, through some secret known to her, Rose's mother had received momentary energy.

"You may be right," Dr. Tiffen said.

"If you think there's something to my theory, I'll try to find that 'source of light,'" the young detective declared.

Before Nancy reached her car, Dr. Tiffen called her back. "Mrs. Struthers is on the phone."

She told Nancy that the police had just notified her that they had located part of her stolen property in a Winchester pawnshop.

"They're holding several suspects and one of them may be the thief who stole my jeweled bag. He may also be the one who robbed the house. Could you go over to Winchester, Nancy, and identify him?"

The girl glanced at her wrist watch. She could just about make it there and back before dark, and thus keep her promise to her father and Hannah that she would not stay out alone at night while working on the Struthers case.

"I'll run right over," she agreed.

For the second time that day Nancy headed her car for Winchester. Should any of the men in the police line-up be those suspected as thieves, she hoped they would confess and clear up a large part of the mystery. Unfortunately she had never seen any of them before.

Early the next morning Nancy received a call from a state police officer. "Miss Drew," he said, "we've located those gypsies. They're on the south side of Hancock. One of the men from the barracks near there will go with you. What time can you reach Hancock?"

"About nine-thirty. Thank you very much."

As soon as Nancy and Hannah had had breakfast, the girl detective went off, her hopes high. Now perhaps she would find Romano Pepito! If not, surely she would pick up a clue to the whereabouts of Anton, Nitaka, and perhaps even Murko. He might tell her who left the blanket with the strange message.

At exactly nine-thirty Nancy walked into the Hancock Barracks' office. A uniformed state policeman named Wicks was assigned to accompany her to the gypsy settlement. As they approached the secluded place, the callers were greeted by barking dogs.

The warning sent gypsies scurrying toward

their trailers. Women who had been cooking meat over brilliant-red fires hastily gathered their playing children and retreated. When the policeman addressed a question to a young woman who hurried past, she replied, *"Ci janav."* He explained to Nancy that this mean, "I don't know."

The same reply was received from other fleeing figures. Evidently the gypsies had no intention of giving any information to the police!

One man did come forward and make a pretense of welcoming the couple. Nancy had never seen him before, nor any of the gypsies who were looking curiously from the doorways and windows of their trailers. So far as she could judge, these were not the people she had visited before.

Politely she asked if Zorus, Murko, Romano Pepito, Anton, Nitaka, Tony Wassel, or Henrietta Bostwick were there. The man shook his head at mention of each name.

"The persons I'm looking for aren't here," she said to Wicks.

"Just the same, we'll make sure and not take anyone's word for it," he replied.

The officer investigated on his own, but came back convinced that the purse snatcher was not hiding in the camp.

"If he was here, he fled before we came," Wicks decided.

Nancy bought a string of beads from a young woman. Then she and Wicks left.

Nancy reached River Heights just as the clock in the town-hall tower chimed the midday hour. She loved to listen to it and often laughingly told Hannah that it made her feel as though the old bell were announcing the end of one adventure and the beginning of another.

"But today it means nothing more mysterious than a luncheon date with Bess and George, and a look at the mannequin doll's wedding party," she reflected with a chuckle.

At one o'clock she met the cousins at the new restaurant Bess had recommended.

"Let's walk to Taylor's from here," Bess suggested after they finished a hearty meal. "I feel ten pounds heavier."

The department store was only two blocks away. George told her cousin she should climb up the five flights to the doll exhibit as well, if she expected to reduce. Bess grimaced and got in the elevator.

The roped off area was already crowded when the girls entered, but they managed to make their way to the front and were thrilled at the exquisite scene on stage. Six dainty bridesmaids stood in attendance on a beautiful bride.

"Did you ever see anything so lovely?" Bess whispered. "Especially the bride! She looks real enough to walk right down the aisle!"

As Nancy gazed at the bride mannequin, her thoughts roved. She recalled the gypsy wedding at the carnival and how the child bride had received a symbolic doll as part of the ceremony. Then she recalled the photograph Mrs. Struthers had shown her of Rose's mother in her white bridal gown.

"Girls," she whispered, excited, "we must go at once to Mrs. Struthers'. I believe I have the answer to the mystery! It's in the old album after all!"

CHAPTER XV

A Detective Fails

BESS and George were startled by Nancy's sudden declaration.

"In which old album?" George asked. "You've uncovered so many I can hardly keep track of them all."

Nancy grinned at her friend. "It's not that confusing, George," she said. "I'm sure we can find the clue in that old album of Mrs. Struthers'."

"The one the precious stones were stolen from?" Bess questioned.

"Right!" Nancy answered. "Let's hurry over to her house and I'll show you what I mean."

The three girls soon reached the Struthers home and hurried inside. While the others watched in bewilderment, Nancy quickly flipped through the pages of the brass-filigree album until she came to the photograph of Enid Struthers in her bridal gown.

"Do you notice anything odd about this picture?" she asked.

In turn George, Bess, and Mrs. Struthers examined the photograph and shook their heads.

"Don't you see anything unnatural about it?" Nancy persisted.

Rose, who had joined the group, volunteered her opinion. "It looks more like a doll than my mommy!"

"Exactly!" cried Nancy, pleased to have her hunch confirmed. "Rose, I'm sure this isn't a photograph of your mother. It's a picture of a doll made to look like her!"

"Why, Nancy, that's fantastic!" Mrs. Struthers exclaimed. "This is my daughter!"

"If you'll look closely at the face, you can see an artificiality about it," Nancy declared.

The others scrutinized the picture carefully, and realized that Nancy was right.

"Such a lifelike doll makes those mannequins at Taylor's look like so many sticks," George remarked.

"But seeing them gave me the idea about this picture." Nancy smiled.

"How do you account for the doll being made?" Mrs. Struthers asked.

"My guess is that Romano, being a gypsy, wanted to follow their custom of presenting a doll to his bride. Since she was not a child and not a gypsy, he had one made to look like her in her bridal dress. He probably thought it so attractive that he had it photographed."

"But why go to all that trouble?" George questioned. "Why didn't he just take a picture of Mrs. Pepito?"

"If I had the answer to that," Nancy replied, "I'd have the key to the whole mystery." To herself she said, "Maybe Enid didn't have a bridal dress of her own."

"What do you suppose became of the doll?" Mrs. Struthers asked. "If Enid had it, why didn't she show it to me or to Rose?"

"Perhaps your daughter was forced to sell the doll," Nancy speculated. "Or possibly her husband took it with him."

"Without doubt this doll in the picture is the one I'm to find for Rose," Mrs. Struthers said. "But what importance could it have for her? During the last few days of Enid's life, she did say she had expected Rose to be well off financially, someday, but that the hope had been lost. Could that have had some connection with the doll itself?"

Instead of answering, Nancy looked at the elderly woman and asked, "Mrs. Struthers, at the time of your daughter's illness, did you have the same servants you have now?"

"No, a Mrs. Hunt was with us then. She was our housekeeper and was very attentive to Enid."

"Where is Mrs. Hunt now?"

"She has retired to a little cottage near the edge

of River Heights. It was through her that I came here. Do you think she might know something helpful, which she did not tell me?"

"Possibly," Nancy replied.

"Then do call on her," Mrs. Struthers said.

As the girls left the house, George and Bess suddenly remembered that they had promised to meet their mothers downtown to go shopping. Nancy dropped them off and drove to the former housekeeper's home alone.

Mrs. Hunt was rather reserved at first, but Nancy's straightforward and sincere manner impressed her. When the woman seemed satisfied that Nancy wanted to help Rose and her grandmother, she willingly told her everything she knew about Enid Struthers.

"I felt so sorry for the poor girl," she murmured. "Her marriage to Romano Pepito brought her happiness for only a short time. She didn't confide in her mother about her fears, but she did tell me a few things."

"Did she ever mention a doll made to look like her?" Nancy asked.

"No, she didn't. If she had one, she probably kept it in a small trunk in her room."

Nancy looked surprised, for Mrs. Struthers had never mentioned the trunk to her.

"Enid always wore the key to it on a ribbon around her neck," Mrs. Hunt added. "She never opened the trunk when anyone was near."

"What became of it?"

"I don't know. Mrs. Struthers may still have it. But the contents are gone. They were removed by Enid before she died."

"Do you know why?"

"About a week before poor Enid passed away, she and I were alone in the house. A woman came to see her. They talked a long while together. Then they went to Enid's bedroom."

"Did Mrs. Pepito seem upset?"

"No, she seemed very pleased about the whole affair. The visitor finally left, carrying a rather large package. After that, Enid never bothered to lock the trunk, and one day when it was open, I noticed it was empty."

"You've no idea what it was she gave away!"

"Not the slightest. For a day or two she was very happy, telling me her broken life was about to be set right. Then, seemingly for no reason, she became discouraged and began to cry a good deal. Her illness, which was incurable, become worse, and she passed away suddenly."

"She said nothing about her visitor?"

"Not directly, but when I mentioned her, Enid said please not to tell her mother anyone had been there."

"Mrs. Struthers told me that Enid on her death-bed begged her mother to find a certain doll. She seemed to want it for Rose."

"Yes," Mrs. Hunt nodded sadly, "but we couldn't figure out what she meant."

"Do you recall what the woman who came after the package looked like?" Nancy asked.

"Yes, indeed. She was of medium height and well dressed. Her eyes were dark and piercing— the kind that usually go with coal-black hair. But this woman's hair I guess was bleached. Anyway, it was a strange shade, a kind of carrot color."

"Oh!" Nancy cried. "I know who she is!"

"You do?" asked Mrs. Hunt, astounded.

Nancy did not say that she thought the caller had been Nitaka, but she was sure of it. The pieces of the puzzle were beginning to fall into place rapidly now!"

"I'm glad you called," Mrs. Hunt declared as the girl announced she must leave. "You're a true friend of Mrs. Struthers' and I can see you want to help her."

"I hope I can."

"Well, I don't mean to discourage you, my dear, but that detective she hired never was able to learn anything about the doll. Nor was he able to trace the woman who called on Enid when I told him about her."

"Mrs. Struthers hired a detective?"

"Immediately after the daughter passed away. He charged her an enormous price, in return for doing absolutely nothing!"

"I hope I won't fail," Nancy said with determination. "By the way, part of my work is to find Rose's father. Mrs. Struthers believes the family should be reunited."

Mrs. Hunt was amazed to hear this, but delighted as well.

Nancy explained. "At first I was looking for Romano Pepito to find out about the doll. Then I came across a picture of him and showed it to Rose and her grandmother." Nancy smiled. "He's handsome and kind looking. Now they want him to join the family."

Mrs. Hunt smiled too. "I'm so glad. Enid was deeply in love with her husband, and I'm sure he must be a fine man. By the way, how is Rose? She was unmanageable during her mother's illness."

Nancy reported the improvement in Rose's behavior and mentioned her talent in music. "I believe she'll be on the concert stage and in movies and television someday," she prophesied.

"I'm so pleased," Mrs. Hunt said, as she opened the door for her caller. "Good-by and come again."

On the way home Nancy remembered that she had promised Hannah to make a trip out to the farm where the housekeeper bought chickens each week.

"I'll do it now," she decided, and turned onto a country road.

Her purchase made, she started down the

steep, high-banked lane from the farmhouse. At the intersecting highway she came to a dead stop to look for passing cars. An automobile whizzed by at high speed, but not too fast for Nancy to catch a glimpse of the driver's face.

"The purse snatcher!" she thought, hardly daring to believe her eyes. "In a black sedan!"

There were no other cars on the road, so she quickly turned into the highway and pursued the man. As she pulled nearer, he must have realized that Nancy was trying to overtake him, for he put on a burst of speed. Nancy did the same.

The chase was on!

CHAPTER XVI

The Television Clue

NANCY became aware of a roaring noise behind her. A second later a motorcycle policeman drew up alongside and motioned her to pull over.

"You know how fast you're going?" he asked. "We got laws, you know!"

Nancy slowed down but did not stop. Pointing to the sedan ahead, which was disappearing from view, she cried out, "That driver—he's a thief! Please go after him! I'll follow and explain."

The officer, not sure that this might not be a way of getting rid of him, said, "Who are you?"

"Nancy Drew. Carson Drew's daugh. . . ."

The policeman waited for no more. Like a released rocket he shot down the road. Nancy, following at top speed, presently saw him overtake the sedan. It pulled to the side of the road and the driver handed the policeman something through the open window.

"Probably his license," the girl surmised.

As Nancy reached them and looked the driver square in the face, she knew without a doubt he was the purse snatcher.

"Mr. Rosser here says he's innocent of your charge," the policeman said to Nancy.

"Rosser? His name is Tony Wassell," Nancy explained.

"Officer, you see from my license what my name is," the man declared indignantly. "I've never seen this girl before, and I don't know what she's talking about. Now, if you're through with me, I'll go along."

"Not so fast," the officer said. "Tony Wassell, eh? That name's in the police records."

"Yes," Nancy spoke up. "He's the man who stole a purse with money and other valuables from Mrs. John Struthers."

"Oh, so you're the guy," said the officer, remembering the case. "And if you're Tony Wassell, you're the gypsy we've got other charges against."

"I'm not a gypsy!" the man retorted angrily.

"Wait until Anton and Nitaka hear that!" Nancy said, hoping to trap him into betraying an association with the couple.

"Anton and Nitaka!" The man spoke the words involuntarily, a look of dismay crossing his face.

"You three work for the king, don't you?" Nancy quizzed him.

The gypsy's eyes blazed. "What do you know about the king?" he demanded.

"More than you think!" she replied. "And you

were so afraid I'd have you arrested, you sent me a warning note, and then tried to shove my car off the road and injure me so I couldn't work on the Struthers case."

The gypsy, still protesting his innocence, was taken to police headquarters for further questioning. There he stubbornly maintained a stony silence. The only time he spoke was when one of the officers asked him if he wanted a lawyer, or would like to get in touch with anyone he knew.

"No!" the thief snapped. "Leave me alone!"

Nancy took Mrs. Struthers to the police station the next morning to prefer charges against him. Even then the prisoner refused to admit anything or tell them what he had done with the contents of the woman's bag.

"He'll talk after he's been here a few days," an officer told Nancy knowingly.

When she returned home a little later, Nancy found Ned Nickerson on the porch swing. He listened attentively to Nancy's vivid account of the purse snatcher's capture.

"Nice going, Nancy," he observed, "but how about playing a little for a change? One crook in jail is enough for any detective! I have two days off at the beginning of the week."

Nancy smiled. "Fine idea! Let's go on a boat ride on the river Monday if it's clear."

"Great!"

When Ned arrived at eleven o'clock Monday

morning, Nancy handed him a tempting lunch hamper. "How about a couple of Dad's fishing rods? Shall we take them?" she asked.

"Swell idea. I'll get them."

Fifteen minutes later Nancy and Ned were on their way. He made one stop to buy bait and in a short time they reached a motorboat rental dock. Ned selected one, and soon the grinning couple were headed downstream.

"Where to?" he asked.

"Dad says there's good fishing in Pilot's Cove," Nancy replied.

Ned turned the boat in that direction and by the time they reached the spot, they were both ready for the generous lunch Hannah had packed. They fished that afternoon and enjoyed competing with each other. When they finally reeled in their lines, Ned had five trout and Nancy three.

"What'll we do with all these fish?" Nancy laughed, as Ned started the motorboat.

"We might call on the Wyatts," he suggested. "They have a cottage not far from here."

"You mean Hazel and Bill?" Nancy asked, referring to a young engineer and his wife, who had been married only a short time.

"Yes."

"I'd love to see them," Nancy agreed.

Ned rowed toward the channel of the Muskoka River. Four miles south, they tied up in front of a small picturesque stone house perched on a hillside overlooking the water. To their delight, they found the Wyatts at home.

"Well, it's about time you came to see us!" Hazel greeted them enthusiastically. "You're staying to dinner too. No excuses!"

"Thanks, we will," Ned accepted. "And here's part of our meal," he added, presenting Hazel with the fish.

For an hour the young people sat on the stone terrace, chatting and sipping frosty cool drinks. Bill spoke of his interesting work in the manufacture of television apparatus and said, "I want you to see our set. It's the last word in television."

"Any good programs on now?" Hazel asked. "This time is usually given over to children's stories. Adult shows come on later."

Bill scanned a TV schedule. Finally he said, "There's to be a Thomas Smith on at eight o'clock. Someone at the studio says he's good. Plays the violin. He has never been televised before."

Nancy was interested at once. "Let's tune in to that program," she suggested.

A little before eight Bill turned on the set. Nancy and Ned marveled at the clarity of the images on the screen and the natural sound of the actors' voices. When the next program came on, an announcer introduced Thomas Smith. The artist walked to the center of the stage and put his violin under his chin.

He had played only the first few notes of the "Gypsy Love Song," when Nancy cried out, "Romano Pepito!"

"You know him?" Hazel Wyatt exclaimed.

"Only from his picture," Nancy answered. "I've been trying to find him. It's terribly important that I talk to him. If I were only at that studio right now!"

Bill jumped up. "I'll call the station and ask that the man be kept there until you can drive over," he offered. "Take our car."

Nancy and Ned waited only long enough to make sure the station manager knew they were en route to meet the violinist. Then, with a thirty-mile drive ahead of them, they set off for the town of Aiken. Two detours and a delay at a bridge made the trip longer than they had anticipated.

"It's taken us an hour!" Nancy said as they alighted in front of the broadcasting company offices. "Oh, Ned, I hope Romano is still here. It will be the best break I've had yet!"

CHAPTER XVII

Double Disappearance

NANCY and Ned were whisked by elevator to the third floor of the TV station. Anxiously they asked for the violinist. Daniel Brownell, the manager, came to speak to them.

"I'm very sorry we could not keep Thomas Smith here," he said regretfully. "We tried our best, but he insisted upon leaving."

'You told him it was very important?" Nancy asked, her heart sinking.

Mr. Brownell nodded. "The only way we could have kept him was by force. Naturally we couldn't do that. He left about forty-five minutes ago."

"I must see him," Nancy told the man. "Can you tell me where he went?"

"Sorry, I haven't the slightest idea. And I'm afraid he won't be back."

"Why?" Ned asked.

"Smith said he didn't want to meet anyone. Acted strangely, as if he were afraid of somebody."

Nancy briefly explained to the manager that it was of great importance to the violinist that she contact him. "Surely you have his home address?" she asked.

"Well, it's most unusual for us to give out such information."

"My father, Carson Drew, will vouch for me," Nancy pleaded. "Our finding Mr. Smith may mean a great deal to his future happiness."

Either Mr. Brownell had heard of Carson Drew or Nancy's sincerity convinced him of her desire to help Smith. He stepped into an office and returned a moment later. In his hand was a slip of paper with Thomas Smith's address. Nancy and Ned thanked him and drove direct to the place. It was a rooming house in a poor section of the city.

"I have a feeling he won't be here," Nancy predicted as they climbed the steps.

Her hunch that Romano had fled was correct. They learned from the superintendent that the man known as Thomas Smith had taken all his belongings and departed hastily.

"He just left?" Nancy questioned the landlady.

"Not ten minutes ago."

"Did he say where he was going?"

"No. I asked him if he wanted his fan mail forwarded and he answered, 'The only mail I want can never come.' Then he jumped into an Acme taxi and drove off."

Nancy and Ned walked to the car. The couple realized that they had to return the rented motorboat and were using a borrowed automobile. Ned felt it would be best to abandon a further search for the time being.

"We'd better go back to the Wyatts'," he said.

Reluctantly Nancy nodded assent. She felt frustrated, coming so close to finding Romano, only to fail.

"He may have gone to one of the nearby gypsy camps," she said. "I'll come back here tomorrow and see if I can pick up his trail."

"You never give up, do you?" Ned asked, patting her shoulder. "That's one of the things I like about you, Nancy."

It was late before the young couple reached River Heights. Nancy slept soundly but was up early the next morning, eager to get on the trail of Romano Pepito. She thought of calling Mrs. Struthers to tell her the latest developments but decided against it.

"No use disappointing them if nothing comes of my hunt," she told Hannah Gruen.

"You're not going alone?" the housekeeper asked, worried.

"Not if Bess and George will go with me."

After breakfast she phoned the girls to ask if they would accompany her to Aiken.

"Sure," George said, and Bess echoed the sentiment.

By noon they were in the small city of Aiken, ready to take up the search for the missing violinist.

"First, let's go to the Acme Taxi Company and see what we can find out," Nancy suggested. "It was one of their men who drove Romano from his rooming house."

"I hope he'll remember where he took his passenger," George said, as they parked the car in front of the Acme office.

Nancy found the manager and asked if he would mind answering a few questions.

"It's okay with me," he said genially.

"Did any of your drivers mention calling for a man with a violin at a rooming house on the west side of town last night?"

"Might have been Gus Frankey. He answered a call from over there. Say, did Gus report in this morning?" he asked, turning to an assistant at a nearby desk.

"Didn't show up," the other replied. "We've phoned his house six times. Wife's wild—says he didn't come home last night."

"Did he turn in his cab?"

"No."

"He must have taken his passenger on a long trip." The manager turned again to Nancy. "Gus probably is the driver you want to see."

"While we're waiting for him, we may as well find a place to eat," Bess insisted impatiently. "I'm starved!"

As the girls walked down the street, looking for a restaurant, Nancy suddenly stopped.

"One of Mrs. Struthers' stolen dolls!" she exclaimed, pointing toward the window of an attractive shop.

Amid a display of fine old porcelain figurines stood the dainty little lady on a velvet box, holding her fan and bouquet. Nancy hurried into the shop. A pleasant elderly woman came forward. At Nancy's request she took the doll from the window.

"Normally I handle only porcelain figurines," she explained, "but when this doll was offered to me, I couldn't resist her."

"Would you mind telling me whom you bought it from?" Nancy asked. "The doll is really a collector's piece, isn't it?"

"Indeed it is. The woman who sold it said she had bought it in Paris. She's disposing of her collection."

"Did the woman have olive skin and carrot-colored hair?" Nancy asked.

"Yes, she did," the shopowner replied.

"Then I'm afraid you were sold a stolen doll by a gypsy named Nitaka," Nancy said, sorry to have to reveal such unpleasant news. "When did you buy it?"

"It's one of Mrs. Struthers' stolen dolls!" Nancy
exclaimed.

"Only yesterday."

Nancy turned to Bess and George. "That might mean Anton and Nitaka are somewhere near here, as well as Romano!" she exclaimed.

The shopkeeper was confused by the girl's reference to persons she did not know. "It never occurred to me that the doll was stolen," she said nervously.

Nancy looked about for a phone. "I think we'd better call the owner of the doll," she said.

"I hope she won't blame me for buying it," the shopkeeper said nervously.

"I'm sure she won't," Nancy assured her. "Mrs. Struthers is very kind. I'll explain everything to her."

Bess spoke up. "You'll probably be hours on the phone, Nancy. Suppose George and I get sandwiches and bring them back to the car."

"All right," Nancy said, and picked up the phone. She placed her call, and presently heard Mrs. Struthers' voice. Instantly she knew from the woman's tone that something had gone wrong.

Before she could mention having found the stolen doll, Mrs. Struthers cried, "Oh, Nancy, the most dreadful thing has happened! I've been trying to get hold of you. Rose has disappeared! We're afraid she may have been kidnapped."

"How terrible!" Nancy exclaimed. "When did this happen?"

"Just this morning. Oh, what'll I do? What'll I do?"

"Maybe Rose went to visit one of her play-mates," Nancy suggested, trying to soothe the woman.

"No, we've looked everywhere."

"Did you call the police?"

"Yes. Everyone is searching for her, but no one's seen her since she went out to play in the yard this morning. Oh, I'm desperate. If anything should happen to that child. . . ."

"Mrs. Struthers, it's just possible Rose ran away of her own accord," Nancy suggested quickly.

"Why would she do that?"

"Rose has talked a good bit lately about going into television and movies," Nancy said. "She may have taken a train to New York to try for an audition."

"Nancy, you may be right. Her violin is gone too."

Actually Nancy did not think this was what had happened. Rather, she felt that Mrs. Struthers' first guess was correct—that Rose had been kid-napped.

After promising Mrs. Struthers she would do everything possible to find her granddaughter, Nancy was in a quandary. Should she go back to River Heights or keep on trying to locate Romano? It was just possible, she decided, that

there was a connection between the two disappear-
ances!

Nancy arranged with the owner of the shop to
keep the doll until plans could be made for Mrs.
Struthers to claim it. Then Nancy hurried back to
the Acme Taxi Company.

As she arrived a dusty cab turned into the
garage. The girl wondered if this could be the one
Thomas Smith had hired. Impulsively she stopped
the driver to inquire if he were Gus Frankey.
When he said he was, Nancy asked if he had
picked up a violinist by the name of Thomas
Smith at the studio the night before.

"I sure did," the man answered. "Worse luck
for me!"

"What do you mean?"

"I'd rather not say."

"It's important that I find Mr. Smith," Nancy
said urgently. "Where is he?"

"You'd need a map to find the place."

Nancy wondered why the man was so evasive.
It was maddening when time was short. Rose had
disappeared, and Romano might be within reach!

"Listen," said Nancy, "this may be a life-and-
death matter. If you don't think I can find the
place where you taxied Mr. Smith, you'll have to
take me there yourself!"

"Hold on, miss. I can't go back there now. I've
been out all night."

"You wouldn't want to be responsible for harm coming to an innocent person—"

The man's eyes opened wide. " 'Course not. Just the same, I won't go unless the company manager gives his okay. I've got reasons."

Nancy called the manager from his office.

"This girl," said the driver, "wants me to make another long trip. I've been out all night and had a tough time."

"It's vital that I find the passenger this man carried last night," Nancy interposed, excited.

"I'll pay well for the trip. But please hurry."

"Take her, Gus," the manager ordered. "You can have time off later."

As Gus went unwillingly to fill the gas tank of the cab and phone his wife, Nancy glanced anxiously down the street for Bess and George. They were not in sight. She told Gus she would be right back, then jumped into her own car and quickly rode around several blocks in the town. She could not find the cousins.

"I can't wait for them much longer," Nancy decided. "Gus may change his mind."

When Nancy reached the garage, she found the girls still had not returned. The taxi driver was fuming.

"If you don't go now," he said, "I'm going home to bed, boss or no boss."

"All right."

Quickly she wrote her friends a note of explanation and left it on the front seat of her car. Then, having asked the manager to keep his eye on the automobile until the girls came, she hopped into Gus's taxi and they rode away.

"How far are we going?" she asked, as they turned into the country. "And where?"

"To that gypsy camp on the mountain south of Aiken," he replied. "And, believe me, if the boss hadn't ordered me to do this, you wouldn't get me near that place with a ten-foot pole! I had the scare of my life there!"

CHAPTER XVIII

An Unexpected Reunion

NANCY was thunderstruck at the taxi driver's words. He had been to a gypsy camp and had had a bad scare! Maybe she herself was running into danger going to the place!

"You took Mr. Smith to a gypsy camp?"

"Sure, and spent the whole night there, too," Gus replied. "When I arrived, a couple of men rushed out and took me inside. There was some kind of feast and they gave me a lot to eat and drink. Then I tried to leave, but they wouldn't let me. I must see some dancing, they said, then eat some more."

"But what scared you?" Nancy prompted.

"The fortuneteller. She told me awful things."

"You didn't believe her?"

"I did last night. Maybe she was wrong, though," the driver admitted. "But I haven't told you the worst part. I can't prove it, but I'll bet they drugged me. I must have gone to sleep while the fortuneteller was talking. The next thing I knew I woke up in my own cab this morning. What I can't figure out is why they did it."

Nancy thought she could. The gypsies were expecting Rose to be brought there! Since the time of the girl's arrival was somewhat uncertain, they had decided to hold Gus until they were sure he would not find out what was going on and report the incident to the Aiken police!

"What became of Mr. Smith?" Nancy asked.

"Dunno," Gus answered. 'Never saw him again."

By this time the taxi had reached a little-traveled dirt road, which led to the mountain. Presently the cab drew up at the entrance to a lane.

"This is as far as I'm going," Gus announced. "You're on your own from here."

"But. . . ."

"Now don't give me any trouble," Gus said grimly. "I'm not setting foot in that camp again!"

"Then wait for me here."

"I'm not waiting either. You couldn't pay me enough to keep me here. I'm going home!"

Thoroughly annoyed by the man's lack of co-operation, Nancy was tempted to tell him why she had come. Before she made up her mind, he said, "You owe me my fare. I got to get going."

"I may need your help," Nancy told him.

"Say, what is this anyway? I didn't want to come here in the first place. If you're afraid to go inside alone, then jump in the cab and I'll drive you back to Aiken."

"No," Nancy decided. "I'll go alone. But please do me one favor," the young sleuth pleaded as she handed Gus the fare and a generous tip. "Phone my father's office in River Heights and ask him to come here at once if he can. And if you see my two friends at your garage or on the road in my car, please tell them, too. Be sure to give them explicit directions, because I don't want to be stranded here."

"Sure. I'll do that much for you, miss. Only don't ask me to come back here. Give me your father's phone number."

Nancy scribbled it on a sheet from a note pad in her purse. After the taxi pulled away, she walked rapidly toward the gypsy camp, which was screened from view by trees.

Finally she left the lane and walked among the trees to avoid detection. Nancy could see people moving about, but thus far her approach to the settlement apparently had not been noticed.

Suddenly a tall, handsome man with a red sash around his waist crossed the clearing. Tucked under his arm was a violin.

Romano Pepito! At last she had found him!

As he entered one of the trailers, Nancy's heart

beat wildly. "This is my chance!" she thought, and wondered how to slip into the trailer without attracting notice.

Just then she heard sounds of laughing, excited children from the far end of the camp. A group, which included several adults, was marching forward. From her hiding place Nancy fastened her eyes on a girl in a gay gypsy dress who was the center of attention.

"Rose!" Nancy gasped as they came closer. "The gypsies did bring her here!"

Much to Nancy's surprise, Rose did not look worried or frightened. Instead, she seemed happy in her new surroundings. Rose grabbed a tambourine from one of the women and started to dance.

"There!" she cried breathlessly, as the exhibition ended. "I can dance as well as any gypsy!"

A fat old woman in a scarlet skirt took Rose by the hand and led her to a trailer that had the symbol of the sun above the canvas doorway.

"You will stay here until Zorus tells you what to do," she ordered the girl.

In her fear of what might happen to Rose, Nancy forgot her desire to talk to Romano. Instead she waited until the group had scattered. Then, when no one was near, she slipped inside the trailer.

"Nancy!" Rose cried.

"Sh! I have only a moment to talk, and you must listen closely!"

"I'm not going back home!" the girl retorted defiantly, as if she had guessed why Nancy was there. "These people have promised to get me into the movies!"

"Please don't believe them! If they did that, it wouldn't be for years and years, anyway."

Rose argued. Nancy knew precious time was being lost. "Rose, have you met your father yet?" she asked to divert the girl's mind.

"My father?" Rose's face was a blank. "No, is he here?" She raised her voice alarmingly.

"Sh!" Nancy warned. "Yes, he's here, and I believe he might leave with us. Come, we'll find him."

Nancy made sure no one would see them. She took Rose's hand and they darted out of the trailer to the one Romano had entered.

Nancy peered inside. The gypsy violinist sat on a cot, his head resting dejectedly on his hands.

"Mr. Pepito!" she whispered, entering with Rose. "I have brought your daughter!"

The man's head jerked up in fright. He stared first at Nancy, then at Rose. As he gazed at Rose, he got to his feet and with a cry of joy caught her in his arms.

"Rose! My little Rose!" he sobbed. "You are alive and well!"

"Father! Don't ever leave me again!" she pleaded.

"No, you and I will stay together always. No matter what Zorus says, we will go away from here." He suddenly realized that Nancy was a stranger. "Who is this, Rose? A friend of yours?"

"She's Nancy Drew and she's been helping Granny find her stolen dolls."

Instantly a look of alarm crossed Romano's face. "Go at once, Miss Drew!" he cried. "Run! You are in great danger here!"

"From whom?" the girl asked.

"I cannot tell you."

"If I go, Rose goes with me."

"Oh, no, please. I have nothing to live for but my daughter."

"Why don't you both go to Mrs. Struthers?" Nancy argued. "She wants you and needs you."

"Never!"

"She has forgiven you for everything, and wants both you and Rose to be with her. Besides," Nancy added practically, "you can use the money you earn to help Rose and stop giving it to Zorus."

Romano blanched. "You know—"

"About the Cause, and Anton and Nitaka. Tell me, why was Rose brought here?"

Before the man could answer, a shout came from a short distance away. Romano turned deathly white. "If we're caught—" He looked appealingly at Nancy.

"Please follow what I tell you both to do," she said quickly. "Mr. Pepito, you stay here until I come back."

She seized Rose's hand, and the two girls left the trailer. "Go to your trailer," Nancy instructed Rose. "Act as if nothing had happened."

"Where are you going, Nancy?" she cried in fright.

"To hide until I can make some plans."

Nancy dodged along the rear of the trailers until she came to one from which she could hear no voices. She took a chance that it was vacant and stepped inside. No one was there. The trailer was attractively furnished with handmade rugs and silk hangings.

A blanket thrown over a bed caught her eye. It was a duplicate of the one that had been sent to her! But the warning and the name, H. Bostwick were missing.

"Maybe this is Henrietta Bostwick's tent," the girl thought. "Who is she, I wonder?"

In a corner of the trailer stood a trunk. As she wondered if any stolen property might be hidden in it, the girl heard footsteps outside. She quickly hid behind one of the silk drapes.

A woman Nancy had never seen came in. She went at once to the trunk, unlocked it, and from its depths removed two dolls. One was Enid Struthers' childhood toy. The other was dressed in bridal garments.

"That bride is the doll I'm looking for!" Nancy thought wildly, as she gazed at the lifelike figure of Enid Struthers.

The woman carefully placed the dolls on the nearby bed. Then she left the trailer. Quick as a flash, Nancy came out of hiding. She snatched up the bridal doll, and then in shocked surprise almost let it fall from her hand.

The figure was as warm as a human being!

CHAPTER XIX

The Source-of-Light Doll

HER MOMENTARY fright gone, Nancy stood lost in thought.

"At last I've found the doll for Rose!" she told herself. "And I believe I've guessed its secret." Excited, she examined the bridal figure of Enid Struthers. "There's something inside the doll that has the same energy-giving effect as 'the source of light.' Some kind of ray, some. . . ."

"So," said an icy voice behind her. "Nancy Drew has learned our secret!"

Nancy whirled to face Nitaka! But the gypsy was not the neatly dressed, tailored woman she had seen on previous occasions. She had carelessly thrown on a gaudy robe and her uncombed hair stood out from her head like a wild animal's.

"Yes, I have learned your secret," Nancy agreed. "Now I will go and return this stolen property to its rightful owner."

165

"The secret belongs to us gypsies!" Nitaka cried. "No one can take it from us! Put that doll down!"

"No, I won't. The doll belongs to the daughter of a gypsy," Nancy countered.

"You mean Rose?" Nitaka laughed wickedly. "She will not need it now. That child will be too busy getting ready for the movies. Then when her grandmother dies. . . ."

As Nancy gasped in horror, the woman added quickly, "Oh, we shall not harm Mrs. Struthers. But she is old, and as soon as she learns Rose is gone from her forever, she will die of a broken heart."

"Then what will happen?" Nancy asked.

She felt very calm now and sufficiently invigorated to carry on a battle of wits against this woman and all her other gypsy enemies as well. Was it a fantastic idea, or was Nancy's strength being renewed by the substance inside the figure in her arms?

Nitaka sensed her thoughts and cried out, "Put down that doll!"

Nancy paid no attention. She must play for time until her father could get there. It would take him over two hours to reach the camp.

Then a sinking sensation hit Nancy. Possibly the sleepy cab driver had forgotten to telephone Mr. Drew! Bess and George? Nancy almost hoped they would not find her. She had a strong hunch that the gypsies would not let her go, and if the cousins should come, they might find themselves in the same predicament.

Again Nitaka read Nancy's mind. "Anyone who gets into the clutches of the great Zorus never leaves," she said, glaring at the girl. "You are a prisoner, and if you value your life you will work for the Cause . . . and gladly!"

"That is how you get your money, isn't it?" Nancy asked. "By threats. But your game is up, Nitaka. You and Anton and Tony Wassell have stolen all the jewels and valuable objects you are going to!"

Nitaka, her eyes ablaze, sprang forward. The enraged woman's fingers reached out for Nancy like grasping claws. Nancy dodged and leaped to the door.

The gypsy cried out, "Anton! Anton!"

The man rushed into the trailer and barred the exit. Nitaka said a few frenzied words to him in Romany, which included the name Tony. Then she hurried outside.

Anton smiled evilly at Nancy. "You will be a pretty addition to our tribe, and a clever one," he said ingratiatingly. "Nitaka has gone to get our king. He will decide what work you will do."

A moment later old Zorus in his regal robes stepped into the trailer. Nitaka followed.

"Ha! You catch this spy at last!" Zorus cried. "But with this girl as one of us, the path of our caravan will be smooth once more."

He spoke in Romany for several seconds, shaking his head so violently his long white hair waved to and fro. Then, looking directly at Nancy again, his eyes narrow and calculating, he said, gloating, "A few more years and gypsies will become all powerful. King Zorus will reign in America, and Anton and Nitaka shall be Prince and Princess of all the people!"

Nancy glanced at his gleaming eyes and knew that the man was quite mad. Undoubtedly he had held sway over his people through promises of riches and power if they obeyed, and threats to their lives if they refused.

What was Nancy to do? Try as she did to calm the three gypsies, her words had no effect. Suddenly Zorus raised his arm in command.

"We go. I do not trust this girl. Her friends may come." More words in Romany, then, "Where we go, she never will be found. Strike out! Pack up! Three cars will go ahead to the mountain hideout. In them will be the three we do not want the police to see!" His laughter sent a chill down Nancy's spine.

Then he gave further instructions in Romany, and left the trailer with Anton. Nitaka grabbed the doll, told Nancy not to dare leave, and went outside. For a brief instant Nancy thought she might escape. She looked out the window and realized the trailer was completely surrounded by Zorus's loyal henchmen.

As Nancy's hopes of help from her father faded, a woman quietly entered the trailer. She looked vaguely familiar.

"Have no fear of me," she whispered. "I'm a friend. Once, when I heard Zorus say Anton and Nitaka were in New York and were going to send you a wicked present, I went to Hillcrest and phoned you a warning."

"The doll with the sleeping drug in it?"

"Yes. And after you met Murko, I sent a blanket with a message. I was afraid for you."

"And you tried to help me when I came to your camp with two girls," Nancy recalled, now recognizing the woman. "You gave me the clue about 'gypsy music fills the air.' But who are you?"

"Can't you guess?"

"Henrietta Bostwick! But that's not a gypsy name."

The woman nodded. "Old Zorus believes me to be one, though. He does not know my maiden name. That was why I left it on the blanket. He thinks that blanket was stolen and that pleases him."

"Why do you stay here?" Nancy asked in a low voice.

"When I was young I ran away to marry a gypsy," the woman explained. "I had to be one of them in order to stay with my husband. I darkened my skin and learned the Romany language so his people thought I came from another tribe. When my husband died, I wanted to run away, but I was afraid. Most gypsies are fine people, but there are evil members in this tribe, and they steal from the others. Whenever Zorus and his helpers plan to harm anyone, I do my best to warn them, as I did you."

Nancy told the woman about finding an album in New York bearing her name, and of the help it had been in piecing bits of the puzzle together. "It was because of the 'source of light' quotation."

"Oh, I wrote that in there one day when I heard Nitaka say it. The album was my mother's. I kept it with me always," Henrietta Bostwick said. "But it disappeared and I believe it was sold by Nitaka."

"Why would Nitaka do this?"

"To raise money. She trades in dolls, too. Sometimes she buys and sells them; other times she steals and sells them."

"But how did you get the two dolls that belonged to Enid Struthers? Didn't Nitaka have them?"

"Yes. But I took them to give them to Rose, to whom they belong. I wanted to leave them in her trailer when no one would watch, with a note to hide them and never show them to anyone."

Henrietta was silent a moment, then she added,

"I will help you now if I can, but we must be very careful. Zorus has ordered this trailer watched. I dare remain only a moment."

"Before you go, tell me about the doll," Nancy requested.

The woman came very close to the girl, and spoke so softly Nancy could hardly hear her. "Some years ago Romano's father found a strange substance at faraway Bear Claw Mountain. Though he was old and infirm, he seemed to feel better whenever he carried it with him. He never told anyone about it except Romano and Zorus.

"When he was about to die, he gave it to Romano. It was at the time that Romano married and was banished. Seven years later, Zorus became leader. He had a mad idea of becoming king of America and wanted to live forever. But Romano would not give him the curative substance, nor would he tell where it was. Finally Zorus had him kidnapped, but still he would say nothing. He has been held ever since by Zorus, under the threat that his wife and child would be harmed if he did not stay with the king and work for him."

"No wonder Enid assumed he had left her," Nancy said. "Does he know she died?"

"Yes, he found out recently."

"And through his art, Romano has brought a lot of money to the tribe, hasn't he?"

"Not to the tribe. To Zorus. The king takes everything. He is very clever. It was not until

Zorus learned Enid Struthers had died that he sent Romano out to play the violin. By that time Romano had no idea where his daughter was and Zorus would not tell him."

"But it was because of the threat to Rose's life that he stayed with the tribe?"

"Yes. Yet, when he heard about Enid's death he threatened to leave. That's why Zorus finally demanded that the girl be brought here to keep him happy. But you foiled the first kidnap attempt."

"Is that why Zorus instructed everyone not to talk to me?"

"Yes, especially people who worked outside the camp, like Murko and Romano. Anton is a good artist. He painted a picture of you and showed it around. But eventually they did get Rose. You know she's here, don't you?"

"Yes. That's part of the reason why I came. But it seemed Romano did not know about his daughter."

"He has not yet been told. There is to be a ceremony to reunite Rose with her father."

Nancy changed the subject. "Tell me, how did Zorus find out where Romano had hidden the strange substance?"

"Quite by accident. He sent Nitaka to Enid Struthers with a forged note from Romano saying that he wanted to return to his wife. In proof of her desire to see him, Enid was to send him the precious substance. Enid then gave her the doll. Oh, Nitaka is clever, but wicked."

A voice from outside the tent suddenly warned that Zorus was returning.

"I must go!" Henrietta Bostwick murmured.

Barely had the woman disappeared when Zorus and four other men came in.

"The girl goes in the first car!" Zorus ordered. "Next Romano. Then the child."

Struggling, Nancy was carried outside. She was bound and a handkerchief was tied across her mouth. Then she was put down on the floor of a waiting truck, with a blanket thrown over her.

With a sinking heart, Nancy felt the truck begin to move to an unknown destination!

CHAPTER XX

Two Victories

FOR HALF an hour Nancy was tossed about on the floor of the moving truck, before she managed to get herself on top of the blanket. But the vibrations and the handkerchief across her mouth made her feel ill.

"Oh, if only Dad could have reached me in time!" she told herself over and over.

Then, just as Nancy felt as if she would faint, the truck halted abruptly. The back door was jerked open, and a man jumped inside. He was a state police officer!

"Here she is!" he cried out, cutting the cords that bound Nancy. He helped the girl to her feet. Then she saw her father, who lifted his daughter out of the truck and embraced her.

"Oh, Dad, I thought you'd never come!" she said, hugging him hard. When he finally set her down, she asked, "Did a taxi driver phone you about me?"

"Yes," Mr. Drew replied grimly. "When I heard you'd sent for me I had a hunch I'd better move fast. I came by helicopter and landed at the Aiken field. On the way I decided I'd better bring the police with me."

"How did you find out where they were taking me?" Nancy asked.

"A Henrietta Bostwick at the camp whispered the secret to me," her father explained.

Nancy told her story to him and the police. As a result, Zorus, Anton, and Nitaka were jailed. After Rose and Romano were found and freed, they went with the Drews. In Aiken Nancy called Mrs. Struthers to tell her that Rose was safe, and to ascertain that Bess and George had abandoned the search for her and were on their way home by train. They had phoned Mr. Drew and learned that he was on his way to rescue his daughter.

Rose and her father rode to River Heights in Nancy's car. The beautiful doll that had caused so much trouble lay in a box beside them on the back seat.

Presently Nancy turned to Romano and said, "Mr. Pepito, before your wife passed away she left a request that Mrs. Struthers find a doll for Rose. Was it the bridal doll, and does it contain an energy-giving substance?"

"It contains a secret substance, which I believe has a curative value. I told Enid never to part with the doll, in case its contents were commercially valuable. Music interested me more than business, so I never investigated it, or tried to find any more of the material at Bear Claw Mountain. I believe Enid must have felt that there might be a source of income in it for Rose."

To spare the man's feelings, Nancy changed the subject and told Romano about his daughter's talent as a violinist and dancer. Rose, in the back seat with him, had not taken her eyes from her father's face. Subdued by her experience, she seemed to have suddenly become a quiet, well-behaved child.

"You're coming to Granny's with me, aren't you?" she asked him, taking his hand in her own.

"You're sure she wants me to?"

Nancy turned and smiled. "Mrs. Struthers told me on the phone she's waiting for you both with open arms."

When they reached the Struthers residence, Rose tried to induce the Drews to come in, but they tactfully refused, and left Romano and his daughter at the gate.

"I'll come to see you in a few days," Nancy told the Pepitos as she waved good-by. "I hope to have a surprise for you then. There's still part of the mystery I hope to clear up."

After submitting to Hannah Gruen's affectionate care, Nancy tumbled into bed and slept for
ten hours. When the young sleuth woke up, she
felt completely refreshed. Bess and George arrived
just as Nancy was getting out of bed.

"So you finally solved the mystery without us,"
said George accusingly.

"Tell us all about it," Bess pleaded. "Weren't
you scared silly?"

"I'm afraid I was." Nancy laughed, and related
the highlights of her capture and release.

Three days later she received word that Tony
Wassell, the last of the crooks to confess, had
broken down that morning and admitted all
Nancy's accusations. She immediately called Bess
and George to tell them, and suggested that they
all go out to the Struthers home. The cousins
agreed.

As the girls rode along, they talked to a woman
with them. No one would have recognized her.
She was quietly and becomingly dressed. Her hair
was neatly arranged and her skin soft and white.

"Nancy, I wonder if Romano will know me,"
she said as the car stopped. "Oh, I'm so happy,
and so indebted to you. I can hardly wait to start
the job you got me at the knitting shop. Here
comes Rose," she added, as the girl ran down the
front walk to meet them.

"The most wonderful thing has happened,

Nancy!" Rose cried out. "My father saw his friend Alfred Blackwell, and he listened to me play. He fixed it so Dad and I will be together on TV!"

"That's wonderful!" Nancy smiled, giving the girl a hug and introducing the woman with her. "This is Mrs. Bostwick. And here are all the stolen dolls," she added, handing Rose a package the police had given her. "Suppose you put them in place for your grandmother."

In the house Mrs. Struthers was talking happily to her son-in-law. She greeted the callers while Romano gazed unbelievingly at the transformation in the erstwhile gypsy woman, Henrietta Bostwick.

"We owe so much to Nancy," he said. "We never can repay her."

"Perhaps we can a little bit," said Mrs. Struthers. "Nancy, did you bring. . . . ?"

From her purse the girl took an envelope the police had found at the gypsy camp, and dropped several sparkling gems into her hostess's hand.

"Choose the one you like best for a ring," Mrs. Struthers directed.

"Oh, no, please," Nancy pleaded. "My reward is in having everything turn out so well."

"You did a great job, Nancy," Bess spoke said.

She began thinking of what Nancy's next case might involve. Bess would have shuddered had she known of the narrow escape her friend was to have in her encounter with *The Ghost of Blackwood Hall.*

At this moment Nancy, quite unaware of this, said to Mrs. Struthers, "These gems belong in the old album. I'd rather put them back there than keep any." She smiled. "Do you know that if Anton had stolen the beautiful old album instead of merely the jewels, I might never have solved the mystery?"

"If you hadn't used the clue in it of the photograph, you would have solved the mystery with the 'source of light' note," said George loyally. "By the way, who wrote that note?"

"Nitaka sent it to Rose's mother after she took the doll," Nancy explained. "It was to notify her the doll would not be returned."

Nancy had brought along a pair of jewelers' pliers and as she prepared to put the gems back into the filigree work, Mrs. Struthers said, "Nancy, I insist you have a keepsake to remind you of this mystery. Would you like one of the dolls?"

"Oh, don't give her that wicked sword doll!" Rose exclaimed.

"No." Mrs. Struthers laughed. "But perhaps Nancy would like to have the fan doll. Would you, Nancy?"

"I'd love it!" Nancy exclaimed. "And I'll treasure it always. Oh," she added, "I have something else for you, Mrs. Struthers."

Nancy opened her purse and handed the woman another envelope, rather mussed but with its wax seal unbroken. The woman's eyes filled with tears as she looked at it.

"The photograph and the letter stolen from my purse!" she exclaimed.

"No one has looked at them." Nancy smiled. "Not even Tony Wassell, who left them in his suitcase at the gypsy camp. So their secret is still yours, Mrs. Struthers."

Order Form
Own the original 58 action-packed
HARDY BOYS MYSTERY STORIES®

In *hardcover* at your local bookseller OR
simply mail in this handy order coupon and start your collection today!

Please send me the following Hardy Boys titles I've checked below.
All Books Priced @ $5.99

AVOID DELAYS   Please Print Order Form Clearly

❑ 1 Tower Treasure	448-08901-7	❑ 30 Wailing Siren Mystery	448-08930-0
❑ 2 House on the Cliff	448-08902-5	❑ 31 Secret of Wildcat Swamp	448-08931-9
❑ 3 Secret of the Old Mill	448-08903-3	❑ 32 Crisscross Shadow	448-08932-7
❑ 4 Missing Chums	448-08904-1	❑ 33 The Yellow Feather Mystery	448-08933-5
❑ 5 Hunting for Hidden Gold	448-08905-X	❑ 34 The Hooded Hawk Mystery	448-08934-3
❑ 6 Shore Road Mystery	448-08906-8	❑ 35 The Clue in the Embers	448-08935-1
❑ 7 Secret of the Caves	448-08907-6	❑ 36 The Secret of Pirates Hill	448-08936-X
❑ 8 Mystery of Cabin Island	448-08908-4	❑ 37 Ghost at Skeleton Rock	448-08937-8
❑ 9 Great Airport Mystery	448-08909-2	❑ 38 Mystery at Devil's Paw	448-08938-6
❑ 10 What Happened at Midnight	448-08910-6	❑ 39 Mystery of the Chinese Junk	448-08939-4
❑ 11 While the Clock Ticked	448-08911-4	❑ 40 Mystery of the Desert Giant	448-08940-8
❑ 12 Footprints Under the Window	448-08912-2	❑ 41 Clue of the Screeching Owl	448-08941-6
❑ 13 Mark on the Door	448-08913-0	❑ 42 Viking Symbol Mystery	448-08942-4
❑ 14 Hidden Harbor Mystery	448-08914-9	❑ 43 Mystery of the Aztec Warrior	448-08943-2
❑ 15 Sinister Sign Post	448-08915-7	❑ 44 The Haunted Fort	448-08944-0
❑ 16 A Figure in Hiding	448-08916-5	❑ 45 Mystery of the Spiral Bridge	448-08945-9
❑ 17 Secret Warning	448-08917-3	❑ 46 Secret Agent on Flight 101	448-08946-7
❑ 18 Twisted Claw	448-08918-1	❑ 47 Mystery of the Whale Tattoo	448-08947-5
❑ 19 Disappearing Floor	448-08919-X	❑ 48 The Arctic Patrol Mystery	448-08948-3
❑ 20 Mystery of the Flying Express	448-08920-3	❑ 49 The Bombay Boomerang	448-08949-1
❑ 21 The Clue of the Broken Blade	448-08921-1	❑ 50 Danger on Vampire Trail	448-08950-5
❑ 22 The Flickering Torch Mystery	448-08922-X	❑ 51 The Masked Monkey	448-08951-3
❑ 23 Melted Coins	448-08923-8	❑ 52 The Shattered Helmet	448-08952-1
❑ 24 Short-Wave Mystery	448-08924-6	❑ 53 The Clue of the Hissing Serpent	448-08953-X
❑ 25 Secret Panel	448-08925-4	❑ 54 The Mysterious Caravan	448-08954-8
❑ 26 The Phantom Freighter	448-08926-2	❑ 55 The Witchmaster's Key	448-08955-6
❑ 27 Secret of Skull Mountain	448-08927-0	❑ 56 The Jungle Pyramid	448-08956-4
❑ 28 The Sign of the Crooked Arrow	448-08928-9	❑ 57 The Firebird Rocket	448-08957-2
❑ 29 The Secret of the Lost Tunnel	448-08929-7	❑ 58 The Sting of the Scorpion	448-08958-0

Also Available The Hardy Boys Detective Handbook   448-01990-6

**VISIT PUTNAM BERKLEY ONLINE
ON THE INTERNET: http://www.putnam.com/berkley**

Payable in U.S. funds. No cash accepted. Postage & handling: $3.50 for one book. $1.00 for each additional. Maximum postage $8.50. Prices, postage and handling charges may change without notice. Visa, Amex, MasterCard call 1-800-788-6262, ext. 1, or fax 1-201-933-2316.

Or, check above books
and send this order form to:

**The Putnam Publishing Group
P.O. Box 12289, Dept. B
Newark, NJ 07101-5289**

Please allow 4-6 weeks for delivery.
Foreign and Canadian delivery 8-12 weeks

Book Total	$ _____
Applicable Sales Tax (CA, NJ, NY, GST Can.)	$ _____
Postage & Handling	$ _____
Total Amount Due	$ _____

Nancy Drew® and The Hardy Boys® are trademarks
of Simon & Schuster, Inc. and are registered
in the United States Patent and Trademark Office.

Bill my: ❑ Visa ❑ MasterCard ❑ Amex _____ (expires)

Card#_____
($10 minimum)

Daytime Phone # _____

Signature_____

Or enclosed is my: ❑ check ❑ money order
SHIP TO:
Name _____
Address _____
City _____ State _____ Zip _____
BILL TO:
Name _____
Address _____
City _____ State _____ Zip _____

DETACH ALONG DOTTED LINE AND MAIL IN ENVELOPE WITH PAYMENT

Southeast

Guide to America's Outdoors

Guide to America's Outdoors
Southeast

By John Thompson
Photography by Raymond Gehman

NATIONAL
GEOGRAPHIC
WASHINGTON, D.C.